Hilary E. Wingate

THE ESCAPES OF MR. HONEY

By the same Author:

WINNIE O'WYNN
SMILER BUNN
PROSPER FAIR
DIMITY GAY
GEORGE H. JAY
THE MIDNIGHT MYSTERY
THE PYRAMID OF LEAD
ARSENIC AND GOLD
THE HOUSE OF STRANGE VICTIMS
THE HOUSE OF CLYSTEVILL, ETC.

THE ESCAPES OF MR. HONEY

An Entertainment comprising the Curious Adventures of an English Author in the Gulfs of the Bygone

By
BERTRAM *ATKEY*

LONDON
MACDONALD & CO. (Publishers) LTD.
19, *LUDGATE* HILL, E.C.4

First published July 1944
Second impression August 1944

This book is produced
in complete conformity
with the War Economy Agreement

PRINTED IN GREAT BRITAIN BY PURNELL AND SONS, LTD.
PAULTON (SOMERSET) AND LONDON

NOTE

Every character in this book is historical, prehistorical, mythological or fictitious. No reference whatever is intended to any living person—except to myself, and what I say about myself is of absolutely no importance.

BERTRAM ATKEY

INTRODUCTION

It has been emphasised to me by many people qualified to judge that these accounts of the amazing adventures of my old friend, Hobart Honey, in what, with his approval, I have termed The Gulfs of the Bygone, are presented in such a very unusual form that a clearly-expressed reason for such presentation is due to those who read or wish to read the adventures.

Few people, I am told, will have read far before they find themselves making the perfectly natural enquiry—"Why did not Hobart Honey, an author himself, personally write the accounts instead of delegating the task or duty to Bertram Atkey? And why was Atkey permitted to air and exercise his peculiar sense of humour to such an extent in his presentation of these startling adventures? Surely"—many will say—"surely a record so unique deserves to be treated with the profound seriousness, even gravity, with which all scientific discoveries deserve to be treated?"

At first glance such people would seem to be right. Certainly that was my view when Honey first broached the matter to me. Very easily, however, my friend convinced me that this view was wrong—as will be seen.

I have faithfully carried out Hobart Honey's explicit wishes—to the best of my ability—and consequently do not feel called upon to apologise for any least suspicion of levity, facetiousness, farcicality, flippancy or even genuine humour which may or may not characterise the narrative.

For many years past Hobart Honey (which, of course, is not his real name—that, for obvious reasons, cannot be given) and I have been close friends. We shared a set of chambers in old Clifford's Inn in our younger days, we explored London together over a long period, we played—and still play—a good deal of golf together, for years we took out a joint licence to shoot in the New Forest or shared the expense of some other shooting together and—when we could afford it—we have made many fishing trips to Scotland together. I am a great admirer of Hobart's work, which is different from and very much better than mine. He is a wiser and much more experienced man than I can claim to be; his philosophy is sounder, more logical and much more impregnable than mine. In the matter of sheer experience of Life and Living neither I nor any other man can compare with him. I am proud to be his intimate friend.

He first began to tell me of his astounding adventures some years ago. In the beginning I was frankly sceptical, and he knew this. But a time came when I believed him unreservedly. He sensed this at once, and it was then that he insisted that *I* should write this book. Naturally I demurred—

"Firstly"—I said—"you, personally, lived through these adventures—you have them very much at your finger-tips, with all their local colour; secondly, you are a very much better writer than I am or can ever hope to be. That, to my mind, is conclusive."

"You miss the point," he replied. "If *I* write an account of these experiences it will be merely horrible—in the main, a series of studies of villainy throughout the ages as we of this day understand the word 'villainy.' It would be too grim—because it would be too true, too real, too sincere and, above all, too utterly unrelieved by any single gleam of humour. No, my dear chap, the man who writes the book must have the ability to present or, if you like, misrepresent almost any conceivable event well-invested with a great deal of robust, coarse humour. Now, *you* can do that sort of thing, dear old chap, to perfection. As for the facts, I shall aways be at your elbow. Believe me, I have thought it over, very long and very seriously. It is the only way—manner—in which to do this book convincingly—no, readably. Nobody is likely to be interested in the long career of a cut-throat unless he is an entertaining cut-throat. No, no, plenty of coarse, common humour is what is wanted—and you are the very man to do it!"

"My dear Hobart, you hand me a very large and acrid lemon imperfectly concealed in silver paper," I said, rather stiffly. "But as you appear to hand yourself a very similar lemon, also, you are forgiven. So be it. I yield cheerfully to your superior judgment and wisdom. I'll do it—and damned be he who first cries 'Hold! Enough!'"

He was so surprisingly and sincerely pleased that I forgot my foolish and momentary pique—and enthusiastically started work on the following day . . .

That is the true account of how it befell that I wrote this book instead of Hobart Honey. Lord knows whether there really is much humour in it. Honey says there is, and is constantly praising the stuff. For myself, I confess that I think he is right when he says as he frequently does—"If *I* had written this in my own way I should have hated myself as I was in those adventures. But you, you crafty old mirage-manufacturer, contrive to make me sometimes seem to be a relatively decent and amusing sort of ruffian. I don't know how you do it!"

I interpret this, coming from Hobart Honey, as praise of a high order. And on these occasions he invariably insists on paying for the dinner, lunch, whisky and soda or what you will.

"I don't know how you do it!" he repeats, chuckling.

Neither do I.

BERTRAM ATKEY.

CONTENTS

THE FIRST PILL

MIRRORS OF GLORY

Mr. Hobart Honey was an English author, a bachelor of middle-age, slightly popular with his contemporaries, extremely popular with himself. He went to India to collect local colour for his next book. And he got it. He got enough local colour to last him the rest of his life and halfway through eternity thereafter. In a bottle.

It was while he was wandering down a side street in Benares that he saw a species of mad dog—either mad, half-mad or just simple—dash from a nearby alley with the obvious intention of biting an oldish gentleman then passing down the sidewalk. With great presence of mind Mr. Honey flung his camera at the dog, who vociferously acknowledged receipt, and, abandoning its vicious design, vanished around the corner, semi-concussed, complaining bitterly about the English and the angularity of their cameras.

The old gentleman proved to be a Lama from the mysterious Forbidden City of Lhasa, in Tibet. In Lhasa there are many Lamas—and they are all supercharged with a wisdom so profound that it looks like magic.

Mr. Honey's Lama was a mild-mannered, benign old gentleman, a little absent-minded, and he was extremely grateful for Mr. Honey's intervention. He *could* have struck the dog stone dead by will power alone—but he never thought of that till long after the dog was fatally scratched by a mad cat up an alley. He warmly expressed his thanks, and after an interesting conversation he went his way. Mr. Honey, completely unaware that he had established a claim upon the gratitude of probably one of the most potent Lamas[1] of modern times, returned to his hotel. That evening a parcel was handed in at the hotel addressed to Mr. Honey. It contained a long letter from the Lama, and a curiously-shaped bottle of emerald-green and amethyst-blue Chinese glass.[2] This bottle contained a large number of ordinary-looking pills. But they were far, indeed, from ordinary—as will be gathered from a perusal of the letter which the Lama sent with them.

Painstakingly translated by an interpreter, the letter ran much as follows:

Inasmuch as thou hast saved me from the Power of the Dog, my son, thou hast established for ever upon my gratitude a claim which shall never be forgotten.

Thou hast said that thou art a common scribe, an ordinary deviser of tales with which to entertain the populace in many lands.

Truly, it meseemeth that thou art over young and but imperfectly equipped for so great a task, for how can thy wandering mind and youthful imagination faithfully portray those things thine eyes have not truly seen, those peoples whose speech thou hast never heard, and those places in which thou hast never dwelt? My son, I grieve for the labour that thou hast expended in vain, lacking true knowledge of the things whereof thou writest. Therefore I send unto thee the means of acquiring that knowledge which is necessary unto thee for the true perfecting of thy craft.

Thou hast lived many lives—thou hast perambulated the face of the planet, Earth, in numberless incarnations. Yet thou hast no remembrance nor any knowledge of these myriad

[1] This Lama's rating (mental) was around 20,000 H.P., though he was quite unaware of it.—Bertram.

[2] Mr. Honey, some time later, refused an offer of £5,000 from the British Museum for this bottle, which was so antique as to be unique—priceless. Later—but not very much later—he accepted £5,005—Bertram.

lives that thou hast lived aforetime—for remembrance and knowledge are locked away from thee and the most of mankind, so that, although thou art a creature of vast experience, thou canst not be, nor ever hast thou been, competent to utilise this measureless and mighty experience in the practice of thine art. Witless, therefore, must be thy works, my son, and ill-informed the boldest flights of thy fancy. It is as if an eagle should set forth to soar upwards unfurnished with wings.

I am full of compassion for thee, my son, for thou art as an Egg which is unhatched or as a Mustard Seed which is unsown.

Yet because thou gavest of thine instant aid unto me in the matter of the dog, I am minded to aid thee in thine art.

So that, henceforth, thy body shall accompany thy mind on its wanderings, I send unto thee the keys of a little number of thy past incarnations. Regard the pills within the bottle that cometh with this letter. When thou art in the mood for education, spend first, as it were, an hour in reposeful meditation, then swallow but one only of the pills, and await peacefully that which will at once take place. Thou wilt return to live again for a space of time some one or another of the uncountable lives which thou hast lived before that which thou art now living. Be not alarmed if thou shouldst awake in the form of a wild swine of ancient days, a lizard of the rocks, or an humble ape bescratching itself on the banyan bough, for thy days thereas will be but brief, and ere thou hast time to accommodate thyself to thy new surroundings lo! the power of the pill shall have waned, and thou shalt find thyself again upon thy couch in these days.

Fear not that thou wilt ever be what thou hast not once been. If, in past ages thou hast been a great king, a noble law giver, a mighty prophet, maybe that the power of the pill will reinstate thee in thine ancient splendour, or if thou hast been before somewhat of an inferior quality, as it might even be no more than a jackass browsing upon the hillside, or a rat journeying darkly through the runs and tunnels of his dismal abode, so mayst thou be again. But what-so-be-it befalleth thee, it is certain that thy knowledge of past things shall wax enormously, and thou shalt become exceeding wise, so that thy fellow scribes, scratching busily like fowls behind the granary, shall behold thy works with amazement!

So much for the Lama. There was a good deal more of it, but the extract conveys the idea tolerably well.

It took Mr. Honey quite a while after his return to England to jack himself up to the point of trying a pill or two. But he possessed an insatiable curiosity, and an extremely good opinion of himself. It seemed to him that when he swallowed a pill he had a glorious chance of finding himself, for a spell, back in the days when he was King Solomon, Julius Cæsar, Richard the Lionheart, or some such notable party. Certainly, there seemed to be a slight risk that he might wake to find himself a two-toed wild ass on a prehistoric prairie, a bat in a belfry, or a stranded jelly-fish drying up on a tropical beach.

"Pity the Lama didn't label the pills," he said to himself, when, comfortably before the fire in his London flat, after a good dinner, he took out a pill and studied it a little wistfully. "It would have been much simpler. For example, 'King, 992 B.C.,' or 'Centurion, Early Roman,' or 'Monarch, Medieval,' or 'Conqueror A.D. 62.' Or if these clammy incarnations had to come into it, a label to each, such as 'Eel, A.D. 1181,' or 'Squid, Stone Age,' would have been very helpful. I should at least know which pills to take, and which to set aside for others. Still, there it is—take it or leave it!"

He drank a glass of port, refilled, and studied the pill. Was that ordinary-looking little thing a free pass to the palaces of Cleopatra in the form of her Roman Heart's-Delight Antony, or was it the "Open Sesame!" to a brief spell of existence as a weevil in a ship's biscuit on board Lord Nelson's old *Victory*?

He might find himself the Great Mogul, T'Chaka, the Zulu King, Jonah, Shakespeare, Dick Turpin, Adam, Oliver Cromwell, or just a galley slave, a baggage camel, a starving wolf, a skunk, or merely a fly in a starving spider's web. He might even be Louis XIV of France discussing, as it were, affairs of state with Madame de Montespan, he might be Sir Francis Drake soaking the Spanish Armada, William the Conqueror, Hercules, Columbus, Lancelot befriending the lovely Queen Guinevere, or any other one of those highly-experienced heroes of Romance.

But at this stage, realising sharply the wealth of pure—or fairly pure—local colour awaiting him, he swallowed the pill suddenly, washed it down with a glass of wine, and instantly wished he had not done it. It occurred to him that he might, after all, have been one of the slightly inferior ones—might wake up as a sixth-century bull-frog baying the moon or wooing a cow-frog in a sixth-century Louisiana swamp.

He tried to rise with the intention of hurrying to the nearest doctor, but he was considerably too late.

A curious drowsy faintness seized him, and the desire to move left him. It was, he thought dimly, like falling asleep with a premonition that one was not going to sleep very long.

This was so.

Consciousness returned to him, as he thought, slowly but surely. He did not hurry to open his eyes, for he felt a little queer.

"Too much of that wine last night," he thought a little muzzily. "Let me see, just what was it that happened? I think—I—was——" no, he couldn't quite remember—something very far-off. He felt a trifle bilious—and the bed seemed to be swaying and rolling like a ship—a ship—why, it *was* a ship.

This was no bed—or if it *was* a bed, then it was on board some ship somewhere.

He was oddly unwilling to open his eyes so he felt himself—a leg, yes, that was a leg, a human leg. He moved it. It was his own leg—good, he was human—a man! He felt thankful—but only in a dim, fading-out kind of way. No recollection of London remained with him—and only one lingering shred of the memory of Hobart Honey—dissolving from his mind like the last wisp of fog in the morning sun. He was like a man waking slowly from a pleasant dream which he could not remember.

But he could feel the heat of the sun on his face. He could feel a fly that alighted on his cheek, and he could both feel and appreciate the sudden waft of air that swept the fly away.

Suddenly he knew who he was. He opened his eyes, and scowled savagely at the extraordinarily beautiful girl who stood close by his couch waving a big feathery fan gently to and fro over his head—a handmaiden.

"Attend to thy task, fool," he said shrilly. "Am I to be devoured of flies because thou art lost in contemplation of some ruffian sailor's tarry knees?"

The girl went white with fear.

He sat up.

"Wine," he said sourly.

She signed to another handmaiden standing close by, apparently for the express purpose of waiting upon him, for she hurried away across the deck of the ship upon which the late Mr. Hobart Honey, of London, had awakened.

And now he was thoroughly awake—as he needed to be, for the Lama's pill had landed him in a period of the world's history when only wideawake men could hope to get on.

The times were rough—naturally enough, for there were a lot of rough people actively engaged in raising roughness to what they evidently regarded as a fine art.

It was, indeed, round about the year 303 B.C., some years after the death of Alexander the Great, when that hard-boiled aggressor, Prince Demetrius, son of Antigonus, had saved Athens from Cassander, whom he utterly defeated. Having no other war on hand for the time being, the Prince had returned to Athens, where he had been giving himself a very hearty welcome indeed—the said hearty welcome consisting of a period of highly riotous living at the expense of the general public, which had not yet realised that Demetrius had saved Athens for himself, not for them.

Mr. Hobart Honey was now Honelius the Eunuch—and until a few hours before he had been none other than Grand Eunuch—so to express it—to the great Demetrius himself—a post, in those days, of extraordinary importance and profit.

Honelius was probably the most successful eunuch of the times—and certainly he was the most crooked. Judged by modern standards, a ball of string was straighter. Even in those far-distant and unfastidious days he was regarded as no gentleman.

Apprenticed to the craft of eunuch at an early age, he had started life in a smallish way in Alexandria, and had slowly worked his serpentine way up in the world until he had been appointed assistant-eunuch in the harem of Demetrius. Many years of success having rendered the kindly old Grand Eunuch, Jorj, careless, Honelius did not find it difficult speedily to direct a fatality towards his chief—into whose sandals he stepped forthwith. For a time he had prospered. He possessed a good deal of low cunning, which Demetrius had once or twice found as useful as some daring beauty on the Prince's matrimonial card-index had found fatal.

But Demetrius, a man of action himself, never had much admiration for his Grand Eunuch or, for that matter, any of the staff of Honelius. As a type, they did not interest the Prince.

This, of course, Honelius knew—and the experienced ruffian did not find it difficult to apply to himself the old proverbs which direct us to make hay while the sun shines, and to paddle our own canoe.

Shortly after Prince Demetrius returned to Athens from the pursuit of the unfortunate Cassander, there arose upon the domestic horizon of the Prince a new star.

She was called Lamia, and it is recorded that she was so devastatingly beautiful that Demetrius fell off his horse at his first glance at her. For her own part, although she admitted that she was no more—nor less—than a simple country girl, who had never before been in a big city, she kept her head extraordinarily well, and within forty-eight hours she was figuring on Card One of the Index of Wives.

This meant that the figures of all the other cards had to be altered—no light task. It was a small joke made by Honelius to the staff of eunuchs as they sat late at night altering the card numbers which made Lamia his enemy for life. It was merely some reasonable wisecrack about ordering-in an adding-machine for the clerical staff if Demetrius conquered many more countries, but Lamia disliked the implication that she could ever be Number Two on the Index.

Honelius had very speedily been informed (by one of his junior eunuchs) of his rocky position in Lamia's good graces.

He checked the lad's story with his usual care.

"Thou sayest she said I was a bald-headed grafter and a snuffy old snake-charmer, hey, boy?"

"Yes, sir."

"Because of that little jest of mine about the cards?"

"Yes, sir."

"Where was this?"

"In her bedroom, sir, this evening."

"To whom was she speaking?"

"The Prince, sir."

"Oh, is that so? What answered he?"

"He laughed, sir—he was in a gentle mood—and said probably she was right. He said he would have a word with thee, sir."

Honelius had turned pale.

"Did he so? And what wast *thou* doing in her bedroom?"

"Gilding her feet, sir."

"Why *thou*? Doing a lady's maid's work like that!"

"The Prince asked that question, too, sir, and the Lady Lamia said she liked me," said the young eunuch.

"*She* liked *thee*! Had she been drinking?"

"Yes, sir."

"Oh, I see. Did'st thou hear anything else?"

The young enunch came closer, looking much more serious.

"Yes, sir," he whispered. "She complained about the quality of the gilding on her feet and the vermilion on her nails, and the Prince promised her two hundred and fifty talents[1] for her to buy cosmetics. The city he had saved would provide it gladly—he said unto her."

The Head Eunuch staggered.

[1] Two hundred and fifty thousand crowns. Demetrius was everything but a small-change juggler.—Bertram.

"How much?" he murmured faintly.

"Two hundred and fifty talents, sir."

"Great Zeus! The Athenians won't stand it. No, boy—they will suffer it not!"

"No, sir."

"All right—thou can'st quit the apartment!"

"Thank you, sir."

The junior eunuch quit. . . .

For some minutes Honelius had sat holding his head in his hands.

The outlook was bad—nay, grim.

This girl, Lamia, was too fast a worker for him. That was glaring—a graven image with its jewelled eyes removed could have seen that at the bottom of a coal mine on a moonless midnight. Here, in five seconds, she had practically wiped him, Honelius, the Grand Eunuch, famous throughout Asia, Africa and probably the rest of the world, off the map, and picked up a quarter of a million crowns for her toilet-table!

She was not safe. Even the brigands of the hills said, "Your money *or* your life!"

This simple country girl said, "Your money *and* your life!"

Honelius thought rapidly.

He must go—yes, he must be getting along. This was no place for a decent, quiet, respectable eunuch. He was not going to be allowed to live—and even if he was allowed to live there was going to be nothing to live on.

He hit a gong and sent a junior for a young seafaring captain to whom he had more than once done the sort of good turn that a young seafaring captain can appreciate.

Then he went quickly to his business office at the entry to the seraglio of the Prince. He had much to do, and very little time to do it in—but he did it.

Eight hours later there sailed from Greece a large caique bearing such a cargo of sheer charm and beauty as probably few ships have ever borne since that day.

Honelius, in his way, could be a fast worker, too.

Within that limited time, working in fear of his life, he had carried out one of the biggest embezzlements of the dangerous times in which he lived.

He had embezzled from the seraglio of Prince Demetrius no fewer than sixty-two wives, viz.—as per Bill of Lading—

> Sixteen Circassians (rich blondes).
> One Delicatessen (Rubens type).
> Twenty-two Georgians (curved ones).
> Eleven Turkish (brunettes).
> One dozen various.

They, too, had heard of Lamia, and they were glad to go. Very few of them had ever seen Demetrius, or ever expected to.

Honelius played fairly fair with them. He told them frankly that he was on his way to Alexandria where he expected to be able to arrange for their marriage to no less a person than Ptolemy, the King of Egypt.

Fond of travel, not averse to adventure, bored with their present matrimonial circumstances, in love with romance for romance's sake, and a little thrilled with the idea of marrying into the establishment of a monarch beside whom even the great Demetrius was a small town hero, the sixty-two leaped gratefully at the opportunity.

It was, as the saying goes, the work of only a moment to falsify the card index. Probably months would elapse before the audit of the matrimonies of Demetrius was made. So, two hours before the sun rose over Athens, Honelius and his plunder were well out to sea heading before a fair wind to Alexandria and—he believed—fortune, happiness, and the favour of Ptolemy, forever.

It was dishonest even then—303 B.C.—it must always be dishonest to embezzle sixty-two of a man's wives. The fact that Demetrius was heavily overstocked with wives made no difference; nor did the truth that the Prince had fallen out of love with the few of them with whom he was acquainted. And the fact that Honelius had about as much personal interest in the ladies as the ladies had in him, did nothing to mitigate this felony. It was just plain stealing plus falsification of the books.

. . . . .

The standard of charm and beauty among the big bevy aboard the caique was naturally high—it averaged round about ninety-five per cent of Perfection, Honelius, a good picker, judged—but even so there was one who outshone them all. This was Icyllene, an oddly-named girl, who was neither icy nor lean. Her origin was completely unknown to Honelius—she always said she had forgotten it. It had been said of her, once, that she, too, was a simple country girl from the other side of the sea. There had been a period when Demetrius had adored her, but she had fallen out of favour—mainly, Honelius had learned, because of her temper. But whatever her temper (which Honelius had found to be no worse than that of an ordinary infuriated tigress) she was a goodly sight—a tall, burning, golden peach-blonde, with great, slumberous eyes, as nearly the colour of violets as eyes can ever be, a figure of such symmetry that Demetrius fell off his horse[1] when he first noticed it, and he was a judge of figures, a smile (when she wished) that would lure young men from the buffet, old men from the counting-house or children from their toys.

[1] Demetrius was always falling off his horse. Drink, probably.—Bertram.

In a good temper she was irresistible—in a bad temper she was like uninsulated electricity.

Honelius did not like her much, nor did he dislike her. He merely graded her as the girl who was the most likely of all his cargo to rank as Morganatic Wife No. 1 pro tem. to King Ptolemy if she kept a level head.

"And take thou heed of this, my girl," he said, interviewing her the day before they reached Alexandria, "a girl in that position can go far in these days. The times are unsettled—the successors of Alexander the Great grab out in all directions for what they can get, and my personal forecast of the winner is Ptolemy. A girl who, so to put it, makes the grade with Ptolemy, and has the cleverness to make me her personal vizier will show the world something the world has not yet seen in the technique of building up a few old-age comforts. Egypt is the country of the future, Icyllene, and thou mightest as well scheme it into thine own pretty little claws as watch someone else scheme it into theirs. Dost thou understand—or art thou daft? Yes? I thought thou wouldst!"

She smiled rather oddly, without speaking, and strolled away.

The Eunuch watched her as she went.

"Now, why did she smile like that?" he thought, failed to guess the answer, and sent for another jar of wine.

The voyage was as uneventful as one could reasonably expect of the voyage of a ship with sixty-two stolen wives, all beautiful, on board, not to mention the handmaidens.

No pursuing craft appeared, bent on recapturing the ladies. Probably Demetrius was too engrossed with Lamia to have missed any wives—or perhaps he was glad of an opportunity to economise.

But, even so, it was with a sigh of relief that Honelius

saw the ship safely anchored at Alexandria. He wasted no time in going ashore and calling at the Eunuchs' Club.

It was early in the day, and the Club was empty.

Honelius ordered something for himself, and invited the Steward to join him.

"The apartments are desolate and the courtyard lone, Steward," he said. "Hath the King departed from the city?"

"Nay, sir—the city is but asleep after the festival."

"Thou art a shrewd fellow, I doubt it not, Steward?" said Honelius, producing a small bag of money. "Could'st use a windfall of Greek gold?"

The Steward looked respectfully surprised that such a smooth-looking eunuch as Honelius could ask such a foolish question.

"No man in this fair city could put Greek gold to better usage, sir," he replied hastily. "I have studied these matters for three score years and I claim . . ."

"Answer me then the questions I shall ask thee and I will set thy feet on the way to Fortune," Honelius interrupted him. "Knowest thou the Grand Eunuch to the King?"

"As well as I know the way from this courtyard to the cellars and back again, sir. Why, is he not President of this Club? How should I not know him?"

"Tell me of him, Steward. Dost thou esteem him to be a man of affairs, quick in the uptake?"

"He taketh all he can get—very quickly, and at all times, sir."

"Hath he a broad mind, or is he, on the contrary, a narrow-minded niggler? Doth he swallow that which he findeth by chance within his mouth or doth he spit it foolishly forth? Is he a partnerly man—content to share good fortune fairly?"

"He is a pliant man, ready at all times and at all costs to augment that which he hath already accumulated."

"That is good, Steward. His name?"

"Pho-Ni—and it is said that he——" but here the Steward broke off very suddenly as a man strolled into the courtyard.

"He cometh even now, good sir," whispered the Steward. "Is it thy wish that the gold of which thou didst speak . . ."

"Anon, anon," said Honelius. "Fear not for the gold. Announce me. I am Honelius, Grand Eunuch to Prince Demetrius!"

The Steward humbly obeyed, and the two Eunuchs exchanged greetings with extreme politeness, eyeing each other intently.

A remote thought worried at the back of the brain of Honelius as he took in the cold, glassy eyes, the thin, cruel lips, the vulture-beak nose and the pendulous jowls of Ptolemy's Grand Eunuch.

"He is no Egyptian, and I have seen him aforetime," said Honelius. "Nay, not this man, I think, but someone like unto him!"

But he could not remember where.

"Welcome to this city, fair Honelius," said Pho-Ni. "It is the hour of the first morning draught—a good omen—Steward, wine to mine own apartment! Do thou accompany me, good Honelius, to a place somewhat more comfortable than this courtyard which already becometh sun-stricken and airless!"

A considerable time had passed, and much wine had been poured, before the sharp-set couple got down to strict business. But when at last they arrived at that stage business was very strict indeed.

As Pho-Ni truthfully said:

"Ptolemy has about as much need of another sixty-two

morganatic wives, so to put it, as I have. He is not like his father—a real ladies' man. He's got a lot of other interests. He's fond of books—talking of founding one of these new-fangled libraries, in fact.[1] His present Royal Wife No. 1 is Berenice, as thou knowest, Honelius, and Berenice is a woman of character. She frowneth upon the morganatic idea!"

"It is then fortunate for our Brotherhood that the morganatic idea has established itself so firmly in the affections of the people and the customs of the kings," said Honelius.

"Sixty-two is a goodly bevy," demurred Pho-Ni,—a good business man.

"Bah! Is Ptolemy the King of Egypt or is he an Arab chieftain in a small way? Hath he—hath *she*—hast thou *no* regard whatsoever for his Glory?" Honelius shook his bald head reprovingly. "How many wives hath he now?"

Pho-Ni took out his wax memorandum tablet and totted up a few figures.

"Roughly, six hundred and ninety! That is not to count the numerous diggers of gold who are hopefully on their ways hither from all parts of the Empire."

Honelius raised his fat hands in horror.

"Six hundred and ninety! Nay, thou doth but jest! Ptolemy Soter the First, Splendour of the East, Total Eclipser of the West, hath but a meagre six-ninety wives to mirror his glory to an awe-struck world! Not even the level fifty score! Tell me, is he a *mean* man—is he niggard of his Treasury? I have not heard so. Six-ninety Mirrors of Glory—for look you, Pho-Ni, what shall a man discover the better to mirror his glory than his wife! Thou knowest —as I know—that the poorest of men is judged by the

[1] The famous library of Alexandria was, in fact, founded by Ptolemy Soter. Where he got the books from it is difficult to say, so the less said the better.—Bertram.

quality of his wife. If she be of good quality doth not the world envy and admire him? How much more so, then, a large quantity of good quality? That telleth a tale—*that* broadcasteth a goodly line of advertisement! But these be but the elementals of our craft, Pho-Ni. Thou knowest! Yet am I taken totally aback, yea, am I bestaggered, at this meagreness. It meseemeth that I am, indeed, arrived in an auspicious hour. There is no far corner of the outer world whereat King Ptolemy is rated a fewer than a thousand wives—not to mention handmaidens!"

"I know, I know," said Pho-Ni, impatiently. "Have I not said that His Majesty is preoccupied with the Library!"

"That, too, is good, and a sign of greatness. But I maintain unto thee, Pho-Ni, that it is less good that he should sink into obscurity with the reputation of being the first known king who stinted himself of a wife or two! Gods! Were such an one as Prince Demetrius King of Egypt I would warrant that a full assembly of *his* Mirrors of Glory would out-dazzle the very sun! Hesitate not, nor linger longer, Pho-Ni! Hasten unto the King forthwith with tidings of my caique-full—advise . . ."

"Nay, there is no need. Have I not had authority these many years to negotiate marriages to any extent on behalf of my Royal Master? Aye, good Honelius, and authority also to debate the marriage settlements with the trustees of the ladies! Art thou trustee for thy bevy, each one of them?"

"Aye, that am I! And because I like thee well, good Pho-Ni—because thou art a man after mine own heart, I am not disposed to be harsh, grasping or avaricious in the matter of the marriage settlements."

They sent for another large libation[1] of wine, and settled down to business.

[1] An Egyptian libation of those days was about equal to what we moderns call a sufficiency or, more probably, a skinful.—Bertram.

"For example, fair Honelius, what might be *thy* notion of an equitable—a fair and reasonable—marriage settlement per lady?"

"A fair question, Pho-Ni," said the trustee of the bevy. "And I will answer thee fairly. An hundred talents for each Mirror of Glory, as to sixty-one of them—noble, beautiful creatures! But as to the sixty-second, the peerless Icyllene—a settlement of two hundred talents will only just save the situation. Less would be to insult the loveliest lady that ever set foot on the shores of Egypt!"

Pho-Ni's face went all wrung-up.

"Gods! Thou art a man with the mouth of leviathan. Dost realise that the sum total of these settlements addeth up to six million, two hundred thousand crowns! Why, His Majesty could build a Pyramid for less money! What art thou, Honelius—a human being or a plague of locusts? Nay,—nay—nay! If we are to talk, in the name of Cheops let us talk as the sane talk."

"Even so, Pho-Ni! I but do my duty as trustee for these fair maids. If the figure I have mentioned grateth upon thine ears make me an offer!"

"Nay, Honelius, for I have no knowledge of astronomical figures."

There was something so firm and definite about the Egyptian's refusal that Honelius weakened a little.

"Doubtless thou knowest the present condition of His Majesty's Treasury better than I. If he prefers to spend his money on books instead of the augmentation of his fame and splendour—but, nay, I find that fantastic beyond belief. Pay me but fifty talents per head for the sixty-one and an hundred talents for the unique Icyllene."

"I will *not* do so, Honelius! I value my position, and I am not desirous to be cast forth into the desert—to the hyenas."

"There would be an honorarium for thee equal to ten per cent of the marriage settlements," murmured Honelius.

"I deal not in vulgar fractions, Honelius. One tenth, sayest thou? I am a fair and a reasonable man. I will take no more nor less than is my fair due—I will give no man more nor less than his fair due. It is just conceivable to the human mind that my Royal master might be persuaded to go so far as twenty talents per marriage settlement per head. And of these twenty talents thou shalt throw back unto me ten talents per lady."

"*Half*, sayest thou!" Honelius choked over his wine cup.

"Fifty-fifty, as the Romans say! Come now, a truce to folly. The marriage settlements shall be twenty talents per head, all in, Icyllene's included—one half to be paid into my hand, one half unto thee. What more just and reasonable?"

"I must even agree. Thou art a hard man, Pho-Ni."

"Nay, but thou comest to Alexandria at an unpropitious hour. The Treasury *is* a little low."

"I am not amazed that it is low, Pho-Ni!" said Honelius sarcastically.

"Be not downcast, good Honelius. Thy share of the settlements will amount to six hundred and twenty talents, and the rate of exchange works out at a shade over a thousand crowns to the talent. At that, thou wilt require a cart to get thy money back to the ship. Another libation? Nay? So be it. I will now view the ladies."

They strolled down to the harbour and the caique-full of beauty.

The last of the ladies to meet Pho-Ni was Icyllene. Honelius, his mind intent on the wax tablets on which he was ticking off the names, failed to notice the sheer surprise which leaped to the eyes of Pho-Ni as the dazzling lady unveiled. Nor did he notice Ptolemy's Grand Eunuch press his finger to his lips as he faced her.

When Honelius looked up Icyllene had already re-veiled.

"Superb! Indeed, thou wert no more than fair in thy description of her loveliness—or of any of them, Honelius. Bid them prepare to meet their Royal husband, and let us hasten to the Palace."

. . . . .

Ptolemy may have had a passion for books but, in spite of Pho-Ni's observations, he was not prone to neglect an opportunity of acquiring yet more Mirrors of Glory.

It was only a few hours after the matter of the marriage settlements had been arranged that he had interviewed each lady but Icyllene, and in each case approved the wisdom of Pho-Ni.

Icyllene, naturally enough, it seemed to Honelius, was the last to be introduced to the King—"the last and the best," murmured Honelius, appreciating the craft of the Egyptian eunuch. Honelius knew that once Ptolemy had recovered from the pleasant shock which the beauty of Icyllene inevitably would give him, nothing remained for Pho-Ni to do but to get the order on the Royal treasury signed, and collect on the same. That seemed to Honelius to be true tact and diplomacy. He had already arranged about the cart to carry his share back to the ship.

The King was in great good humour as Icyllene, fully veiled, glided up to the throne between the two kneeling eunuchs, faced the smiling King, and, in one movement unveiled.

The King looked.

Then his face changed.

He leaped to his feet with a shout.

"Thou! *Thou!* Nekhet! Thou wild-cat again! How daredst thou return unto Egypt! Gave we not fifty talents to our friend Prince Demetrius to take thy fatal beauty and thy cobra temper off our Royal hands but two years gone? How camest thou hither?"

He glared at Icyllene, who glared back. He shifted his glare to Honelius and Pho-Ni!

It was Pho-Ni who spoke.

"Oh, Splendour of the World," he said. "It was this villain calling himself Honelius who conveyed her hither. He announced that he brought the Brightest Mirror of Glory in the whole planet Earth—so fair, so dazzling, so all-but-unbearably beautiful that he would not by any means permit her to unveil. 'None but the royal eyes of the Light of Egypt shall see her first unveil,' said he. Nor could all mine art dissuade him."

The King clapped his hands in a peculiar manner, and a couple of black eunuchs, each about seven feet tall, strode into the hall. They were heavily armed.

Honelius knew why this lethal-looking couple had been sent for. He knew, too, that if these were not enough to deal with him there were plenty more like them not far away.

Pho-Ni had—for no reason known to him unless it was that he meant taking all the marriage settlement money for himself—condemned him to certain death. Dimly he remembered, as he grovelled, hearing that, some years before, Ptolemy, exasperated at the impossible temper of a completely untamable beauty called Nekhet, had presented her to a royal friend with his compliments and a huge present. But who would have dreamed that Nekhet was Icyllene?

"Slay him!" ordered the King, and glared at Icyllene

as if he would shortly order a similar hasty despatch for her.

But Icyllene smiled contemptuously.

"Thinkest thou to order me, also, to be slain?" she asked. "Thou hast forgotten the warning of thine astrologers, oh Ptolemy!" she said icily.

The King started like a man who has remembered something worth starting about.

The lovely liquid voice of Icyllene rose on the silence.

"Thou hast forgotten, Ptolemy—thou wert ever forgetful. But I forget not. Hearken unto me—these were the words of the astrologers as they read them from the stars so clearly that it was as if they were written in letters of light across the whole arch of the firmament: 'Set this woman aside, Great Ptolemy, as thou desirest it, but slay her not, for it is written that when she has been dead in Egypt one day then thou diest also! For thy span is one day longer than her span—and no longer!"

She laughed.

"Rememberest thou not?"

"I remember."

"Slay *me* also, then," she challenged.

"Not so," said Ptolemy, very quickly. He used only the best astrologers, he paid them well, and, as was the custom of those days, he believed everything they told him.

"Nay? Send me again from thee, then, with gold for a gift to make me acceptable—as thou did'st heretofore!"

Her voice was music.

The King fidgeted.

"It was thy temper—thou wert too terrible in thy fiend-furies, Nekhet. Was I not ever tender unto thee until thy furies and hysterias hounded me to—ingratitude and harshness?"

"I have outgrown the period of fury and hysteria, Ptolemy!" she cooed.

The King stared, and stepped down from his throne.

"Sayest thou so, Nekhet—sayest thou so?" he murmured.

She was moving nearer to him.

"If that were so . . . . Nekhet, thine image hath lingered in loveliness within my heart for these two years—and——"

He seemed suddenly to realise that they were not alone, and made a swift gesture.

They were alone instantly—rather quicker than that, the big black guards hauling Honelius along the marble floor at such a speed that the friction hurt.

Outside, Pho-Ni halted them.

"Honelius," he said, "I have waited long for this day. Dost thou remember one Jorj, a fat, not unkindly, old man, who was once Grand Eunuch to the Prince Demetrius? A man whom thou hadst slain by stealth that thou shouldest succeed him. I see that thou dost. That old man was kinsman to me—close kin, Honelius, thou slayer!"

Honelius stared at the glassy eyes, the thin, cruel lips, the vulture-beak nose of the Egyptian eunuch, and knew it would be waste of breath to answer.

"Take him away and slay him!" said Pho-Ni. "It was the order of the King. Be swift!"

Honelius felt the heavy hand of one of the guards drop on his shoulder . . . and it was quite a few seconds before Mr. Hobart Honey realised that the weight on his shoulder was not that of a giant eunuch's hand in Ptolemy Soter's palace but merely that of his black cat, Peter, who often sprang to his shoulder from the arm of his chair.

But Mr. Honey was in no mood for cats just then, and Peter was dropped to the floor with a certain abruptness.

Mr. Honey stared at the Lama's bottle of pills with extreme distaste for some moments, and then reached for the decanter.

"Well, if that's the sort of man I was in 303 B.C.," he said sourly, "I can only say that I am pretty damn glad it's the twentieth century! I knew they were tough in those days—but not all that tough. Either I've improved on myself a good deal since then, or the Lama got his pills mixed. Must try another some time—but not to-night—no, somehow not to-night."

COMMENTARY
ON
THE ADVENTURE CALLED "MIRRORS OF GLORY"

It was only with considerable hesitation that I gave the account of his adventure as Honelius the Eunuch to my friend, Honey, to read, and perchance approve.

Greatly to my astonishment he was—or professed to be—charmed with it. Certainly he laughed a good deal as he read it.

"Yes, I was right to urge you to write these things," he said. "There are, of course, many gross exaggerations, mistakes, and so on, but, compared with the human crocodile I really was when I was Grand Eunuch to Demetrius, you have depicted me as, considering the times, not half a bad fellow—as fellows went in those days, of course. A business man, one might say, fighting fierce competition. That chat I had with the junior Eunuch seems, in the story, very amusing, very. Compared with what it really was. I wish you had described Lamia a little more fully. But, of course, you never saw her. She was too brilliantly lovely to be true! Icyllene was wonderful—a girl *had* to be wonderful to please Ptolemy—but Lamia was—as *you* would say—completely out of Icyllene's class."

His eyes grew blank and his voice absent, like that of a man thinking aloud.

"I was wrong, of course. I should have placated her—flattered her. Not run away. That was a mistake," he muttered. "And, as I see now, it was a bad mistake to have old Jorj killed. A little patience—another year or so, and he would have been pensioned off. Demetrius was not the prince to keep slack eunuchs. Hardly blame him. . . . No, it was my own fault—though, after all, it was millions to one that Pho-Ni should chance to be a relative of old Jorj. In a way there was a poetic justice about it. The pitcher went to the well once too often. Icyllene was cleverer than I believed her—much. And, in the circumstances, Pho-Ni was easily more than a match for me. Yes, Bertram shows that very clearly."

His eyes cleared.

"Excellent, old chap, excellent. I like your description of my pillage of the harem as 'embezzlement.' And the Eunuchs' Club in Alexandria. Actually, of course, there was no Eunuchs' Club at that period. We all hated each other too much—jealousy, a form of jealousy, I fancy. We were a worthless lot really. No real self-respect, I suppose. I don't know—we were quite different from the ordinary man of those days. Thought differently—acted differently. Something lacking, I imagine. It was a wretched incarnation, that. But so it goes. Have a drink?"

I had one.

BERTRAM.

THE FOURTH PILL

KING'S ARCHER

THE next two pills taken by Mr. Honey were, he considered, of no value. One landed him back into an incarnation that must have occurred millions of years before, in which he functioned inactively as a large limpet upon a rock. Throughout this incarnation he never saw a man, woman or child. He never heard a sound but the sound of water moving up to him or sinking away from him, according to the state of the tide. In summer the sun half-grilled him throughout the day, the water cooled him again at night; in winter the frost half-froze him throughout the day, in the usual manner of frost, and the water rendered him just a trifle chillier at night. He rarely left home, in spite of the climate. Occasionally he would unclamp from his rock at night and travel a yard or two in search of a meal or a love affair, which usually began with a fight with a rival he-limpet. But dawn never failed to find him back at home, and probably glad to get there. He would wearily clamp himself down again and spend the day sleeping and thinking. What he thought about was probably food and love affairs and fights with other he-limpets. Irish, one fancies. In the end he was eaten by a superb specimen of the Great Chisel-beaked Auk—now extinct.

The third pill landed him back into a quandary or dilemma. He never knew what he was, where he was or why he was. He spent this life entirely in the dark, motionless. Some sort of bacillus, probably. Again, he was, on the whole, glad to get back to London. He waited some days before trying another pill—during which time he seriously contemplated writing to the Lama and complaining about it. Unfortunately the Lama had omitted to attach any address to the letter accompanying his gift. . . .

Then came an evening when, sitting at ease after dinner, he finished his second glass of port, pushed away what remained of the walnuts, and lit a cigarette. He had worked hard that day, he had enjoyed his dinner, and now he was in the mood for relaxation and entertainment.

He glanced at the clock with some notion of going to his club or a theatre, but at that moment a wild swirl of hail spattered against the window, and the wind rose to a wolf-howl that reminded him with great suddenness of the kind of night it was.

He swiftly abandoned all idea of leaving his fireside that evening, glanced at the Lama's bottle of pills on the mantelpiece, then shook his head.

"No. The old man meant well, no doubt, but I don't think he quite realised what a series of nightmares he was giving me! I've had pretty nearly enough of my past incarnations. What do I get out of it all? An ingrowing inferiority complex in this life—and usually a violent death at the end of every incarnation I return to! It's not good enough!"

He took another glass of wine. It was very comfortable in the book-lined study—the port was good, his digestion was perfect, the fire was cheering, and the purring of Peter, his black cat, was pleasantly sleepy—though he did not feel in the least inclined to sleep. Moreover, the conviction that once upon a time he had been one of the Great Ones of the earth stubbornly persisted within his spirit.

It was true, he mused a little wine-ily, that so far he had not yet picked on the pill that took him back to anything particularly glorious, but, damn it all, he couldn't in *all* his numberless incarnations have been so low that, practically, he scraped along the ground as he walked. The law of averages forbade it.

"I must have been a Somebody sometimes—that stands to reason!" he argued, testily, rose abruptly and took the pill bottle.

"After all, it may be my lucky night! And it's childish to own such a Road to Romance and never use it! So—here goes once more! After all, a man must do something after three glasses of port!"

He swallowed the pill, regretted it—as usual—and sat down to experience yet once more the familiar feeling of swiftly-falling darkness, the brief unconsciousness which preceded his temporary return to some life he had lived before, and the unpleasant minutes of chaotic thought which heralded his awakening.

A slightly dizzy faintness seemed to seize him, gluing him to his chair—and it was growing dark, except only for the warm red glow of the electric fire before which he was sitting. Although the room about him was much darker the fire, on the contrary, seemed to enlarge itself and become brighter. Queer, that, he thought a little confusedly till, almost immediately, his head cleared and he perceived, dimly, that although he certainly was sitting at a fireside it was many sizes larger than that from which the Power of the Pill had removed him mentally and physically. It was at this point that all recollection of Hobart Honey, his works and his possessions left him.

The fire before which he now sat was enormous, fuelled by several oak logs each as thick as a man. A huge pot hung over this fire suspended by a chain. On roasting jacks facing the blaze were the carcasses of a young pig, a number of fowls and half a deer. They smelt well.

He discovered himself to be in a big, dimly-lit, unceilinged, high-roofed hall, full of rough-hewn, smoke-blackened oak beams and pillars. He was holding in one hand a half-gallon leathern cup of wine, and in the other an arrow a yard long. And he heard himself talking, hoarsely.

"Nay, boy,—I swear I have seen snakes that are straighter than this arrow—sharkskin that is smoother—and look'ee, thou poor loon, thou hast even feathered the shaft with heron feathers! . . . The grey goose—the grey goose feather, Dickon, thou oaf! Have I not talked myself hoarse many an hour instructing thee and thy like that never was arrow made to match the grey goose shaft? Foh, thou art a nit-pate—one who thinketh to make jest of the old and experienced, thou sucking babe—get thee gone, young Fat-wit, and straighten thy shaft, polish it, refeather it, and then burn it! Ho, Simon, give me another sip of thy Malvoisie!"

An oldish man, who looked as if he had been a cellarer for a hundred years, rose and took the great leathern jack.

"Nay, Rhobart, the lads were but settling a wager—yester e'en they shot a heron with a few feathers that, being plucked and trimmed, so close resembled thy grey goose feathers that they swore even thou wouldest fail to distinguish one from the other. They wagered among them—was it not so, Dickon?—nay, the lad has gone. . . ."

"Wisely he went," roared Rhobart, "or I warrant thee, good Simon, I would have cracked his young mazzard!"

He took a pull at the replenished jack and stared at the roasting pig with a certain melancholy.

"We grow old, Simon,—it is a sign that one is growing old when these young pups think it good to sharpen upon us the dull edge of the ancient jokes they have but just discovered."

The old cellarer put away a pint of Malvoisie without drawing breath before he answered.

"Yes. It is the truth. Old—old," he muttered, wagging his grey whiskers. "Yet, old though we be—hey?—there is none of these younglings in this land fit to draw us a quart. For I am yet the greatest Cellarer of these days—even as thou, Rhobart, the King's Archer—art the greatest Bowman! Yet well I know, as thou knowest, that there are those who speak of us as two boozy old grandsires who rise from their beds but to sit by the fireside and maunder . . ."

"Let me but hear but the very ghost of such a whisper and I'll warrant ye that nothing more shall pass from the mouth of the utterer but blood!" swore Rhobart.

He dropped his voice.

"Yet it is true we do not grow younger, and the times lay heavy upon us, Simon. These Norman swine flourish and thrive upon their English loot. Even now the Red King carouses with his favourites—upon one of whom he hath newly-bestowed the estate in Boldre Purlieu that once was mine! Not far from here, Simon—as thou knowest."

"Aye, well do I know it!" muttered the grey-whiskered, purple-nosed old cellarer.

"The King's Archer, they call me, true—and that am I, true again, who once was an English landowner in my own right! Yet they might as well call me the King's Clown, for mark'ee, Simon, it is but as an exhibition for his vampire Norman friends that he useth me. As he may send for a juggler or a minstrel to entertain his roistering friends so he sendeth for me. And his look when I have shown them somewhat with the bow is the look of one who says, 'See this curious beast which I have tamed to entertain thee!' As one might speak of a dancing bear! Not thus was it in the days of Hereward the Wake when we sent the shafts humming across the fenlands blood-hungry for the black hearts of the Norman thieves that swarmed like the carrion crows of the saltings . . ."

"Nay, not so loud, Rhobart . . ." Simon broke off as a tall, lean, ragged lad slid stealthily into the big room, glancing about him with quick, wary eyes.

He saluted the red-faced, corpulent old archer, respectfully.

"Why comest thou, nephew?" asked Rhobart, leaning forward in his chair.

The youth whispered urgently for some minutes, and the face of the King's Archer went dark and ugly as he listened, without comment, to the end.

The boy finished his whispering on a long, indrawn breath, and the Bowman passed him his wine jack.

For some moments he stared silently into the fire.

"Mine own brother—Aelfred the Sightless—made blind by William's men—now killed by the men of Rufus! And the little maid, my niece, taken away by Malaise. Whither went she, Edwin?"

"They say that Malaise brought her here on his way to Boldre," said the boy wretchedly, for he spoke of his sister, Edyth, niece to Rhobart.

The Bowman's eyes had become bloodshot, and his voice, soft and purring now, was less attractive than when he bawled.

"Give the lad wine and food, my Simon, he hath come far and fast through the Forest to-night."

The boy ate voraciously at the long narrow table, while Rhobart and Simon talked in low voices.

"Ill news indeed," said Simon.

"Aye!"

"If an old man can aid thee . . ."

"Nay, Simon. With this news I deal alone! Yet I will share it with thee. Here we sit, thou and I, in the servants' part of the King's House—the King makes merry with his friends and, of these, there is one whom he is especially desirous to honour. That is Sir Mors Malaise, the Norman thief, upon whom he has bestowed the Manor which was mine. But the Norman hath an appetite—he must have more. And he hath taken it. He hath taken her—Edyth, my niece, only daughter of my brother—he hath taken her and brought her in to the King's House this even. Doubt not that she sits beside Malaise through the carouse even now. He would exhibit her—God's wounds, there is no such maid within or without the Forest! I have not seen in all the lands of my travel another maid of such beauty, nor of such an innocent and haunting charm!—she is in the grip of this Norman boar! He charged Aelfred, that blind, peaceable man with the utterance of black treason, and killed him. But it was for the maid, Simon . . ."

A Norman officer of the Court thrust his head into the room.

"The King's Bowman to the banquet hall for the entertainment of the King's guests!" he bawled. "Speed ye, Archer—my lords are in no mood to linger on thy coming!"

"Speed thyself to Hell and beyond it, thou bawling bastard!" growled the Bowman. "Lest I give thee that through thy brazen gullet which will fit thee right speedily for thy destination!"

The officer glared and went away. Few people cared to quarrel with old Rhobart.

He rose and crossed to a cupboard from which he took two bows—one an enormous longbow of English yew, shining blackly with use and greasing and careful polish, the other a short, strongly-built Turkish bow, oddly and beautifully inlaid, with up-curving horns.

Simon watched him a little anxiously from under his brows.

"Thou takest the longbow?" he asked, for Rhobart usually did his indoor tricks with the small bow.

"Yea, mine old gossip," said the Bowman. "There is a new trick that I have conceived—and it needeth a bow of English yew!"

He strung the great bow.

"Give me a cup of thy best, Simon, and I will unto my parlour tricks!"

Simon brought the wine, staring yet more anxiously.

"Thou hast a new trick, Rhobart?" he said, and hesitated a moment before he added in a whisper, "It is in my mind that this is a perilous trick—maybe *too* perilous! Have a care, Rhobart—for we be old friends cleaving together in strange and ugly times and it would but ill befit my few remaining . . ."

The Bowman dropped a heavy arm round the shoulders of the old cellarer.

"Nay, Simon, have I ever failed a trick within thy memory?"

"Thou old boaster!" said Simon with a peculiar querulous affection. "I know. It was a qualm—when I saw thee supplement thy Turkish bow with that great, black blood-drinker . . . it was a passing qualm! No more than that! . . . Go then, perform thy tricks, and come quickly back lest the supper meat is overdone!"

Rhobart waited only to whisper a few urgent words and to select with great care the arrows he needed.

. . . . .

Even as he rolled into the great banquet hall Rhobart perceived that it had been a great feast. Half of the guests of King William II were drunk, and the rest were half-drunk. It was a general custom of the period, and a particular custom of the night before any one of Rufus's wild day's hunting of the New Forest stags. Nobody ever noticed his neighbour's condition on these occasions—nor his own. Drink was like the English weather—it occurred in large quantities. There were plenty of ladies present—but of these the old Bowman noticed only one. That was a pale, beautiful child sitting next to a big, black-browed, barrel-bodied man with pale, stone-grey eyes, and a savage face—Mors Malaise, rumoured to be one of the richest, known to be one of the cruellest of the Normans then in the Red King's favour. No doubt he had ministered generously to the avarice for which Rufus was notorious—though, men said secretly, there was little love lost between them.

He had seen the girl, by chance, and, as was the custom, forthwith taken her by design. That was the conquering invaders' way—even in the year 1100.

Rufus was far gone in his cups, and he hailed Rhobart with what he doubtless conceived to be geniality.

"Ho, Bowman, thou English hog, if thou art for once sober enough to stand, show us again thy usage of the bow! My lords, look well, for by the splendour of God, there lives no archer that can outshoot and out-trick this sullen English wine-vat, save only myself!"

He was a fine bowman himself, as he claimed, but he was out, and far out, of the class of Rhobart. But nobody cared to contradict him. The kings of that period were highly impatient of contradiction.

Rhobart noted the rush of colour to the face of the lovely girl by Malaise as she recognised him.

"Ah, my pretty one, thou knowest!" he muttered, set aside his longbow and fitted an arrow to the Turkish bow.

For half an hour he entertained them to an exhibition of trick and fancy shooting that would have staggered those who had not seen him shoot before, if they had not already staggered themselves.

He shot arrows gently into the air which sailed over in arcs and transfixed articles of food on the long table he faced; he shot an arrow to stick into the roof overhead, dislodged it with another arrow, dropped the bow and caught an arrow in each hand as they fell; a score of such tricks he performed, ingenious, fanciful, but each a marvel. Even the glazing eyes of Rufus brightened as he watched, and at the conclusion of his last bit of jugglery with the Turkish bow the King exploded in a muzzy oath.

"By God, I could but barely have bettered that myself," he shouted.

Then Rhobart set aside the small bow and took the great English longbow.

"For my last trick, my Lord King, I will show a new thing which I have conceived and mastered," he declared.

The hall of people watched with a drunken fascination as he walked to a serving table, took butter and rubbed it carefully on the side of one of the smooth pillars of ancient oak supporting the roof. He was minutely painstaking in all his preparations. High on the wall behind the King's table he hung a glove. Evidently he intended to shoot an arrow to glance off the pillar at a wide angle and pin the glove. It looked impossible.

Then he took up his stand. Many minute shifts he made before he was satisfied, and very carefully he examined and re-examined bow-string and arrow.

"In God's name, do thy trick ere we fall asleep, thou fiddling fool!" snarled the King, suddenly tiring of what he evidently considered pure showmanship.

"It is a glancing shot calling for the greatest precision and the utmost nicety of my genius, my Lord King! Yet—at thy command to hasten . . ."

He shifted his feet a fraction, faced the greased pillar, raised the big bow and slowly drew the arrow back—back —back to the very head.

It leaped from the loosened string with a hornet hum that was like a hoot, struck the pillar, flashed from it at an angle, and quicker than the eye could follow it, crashed through the throat of Sir Mors Malaise where he sat, and drove into the wall beyond with a thud—three feet below the glove.

Malaise pitched across the table with a dreadful sound.

The hall boiled as they rushed to raise the dead man.

The girl rose, crying out, recoiling. She caught her uncle's eye and understood his lightning signal to a door. She ran to it and passed through—into the arms of an old, grey-bearded man who smelt of wine.

"This way, child," he said—and she went with him.

She heard, as she went, the shouting die down suddenly —stilled by the voice of the King as he bellowed for silence.

"Thou fool—thou boasting, pride-puffed, barbarian English drunkard! Thou shalt die for this!" he shouted.

"My Lord King, if thou hadst not commanded that I should hasten my preparations all would have been well!" returned the Bowman.

The King stared—seeming struck by the answer. "That is a true word, Bowman!" he said, loudly and harshly. "I hastened thee—and for that thou shalt live—if thou canst. But, by God's splendour, thou shalt not live in quiet content. Thou shalt be outlawed—wolf's-head shalt thou go, and every man's hand shall be against thee. I will have lopped off every arm raised to succour thee during thy few remaining days! From the next rising of the sun I pronounce thee outlaw! Get thee gone!"

Rhobart took his bows and went—back to Simon the Cellarer.

He had several hours before he must leave the King's House—but he must be far on his way before dawn, for there were plenty ready and willing to gain the customary reward that presentation of his head would earn for the winner.

"The children, Simon?"

"All is well—they are already well launched to safety. I have sent them to a relative of mine on the Welsh border. My son, Wulf, goes with them. They are mounted and well provided. Fret not for them, Rhobart, they are well assured. But for *thee*—there is much to do, and little enough time wherein to do it. Eat and drink, Rhobart—all is ready for thee. . . ."

The old man bustled about the table.

"Oh, my Rhobart, that was well done! Well done, though it may cost thee dear. An accident—oho! Thought the King so!" Simon chuckled savagely. But not for long.

"But when he is sober and has talked with others there will be no more talk of accidents!" he whispered. "They will remember that there are never accidents in thine archery!"

He stared bleakly before him.

"It is a blade to my heart, old comrade, but thou must be far from here before daybreak."

The Bowman reached for more venison.

Simon took up a flagon, old, encrusted with cobwebs, and his rubicund face lit up.

"The very best, Rhobart—from the King's own store!" whispered Simon.

"This we share! Death to the invader!"

. . . . .

It was high noon next day in the Forest. The outlawed Bowman was moving north-west from the King's great hunting lodge—and he went as quietly as a suspicious fox. Those were evil days for outlaws.

The old Englishman had no illusions about himself. The Forest to-day was full of enemies—King's men, hungry as hounds, for Rufus was hunting the deer to-day. He must rely on his deadly, his priceless and carefully cherished skill with the bow; his minute and perfect knowledge of the great Forest in which he had been born; his native wit and his experience of men and life.

He walked in the shadows, silent, little more than a shadow himself—but a formidable one.

He was depressed, bitter and sorrowful.

His brother was dead—and he had been avenged. But vengeance could not bring back the man he had loved. His niece had been for a little while the prey of Malaise.

For himself, he was homeless. He had not decided yet whether he would make for Wales—or perhaps Cornwall—and trust to his uncanny skill in archery to establish him, or whether he would haunt the Forest as a lone outlaw—or join one of the many bands to be found.

These were the problems he pondered as he went down the slope of Castle Malwood Walk.

But he had not to ponder them long.

A sudden drumming of swift hooves checked him suddenly by a great oak tree at the side of a small glade.

"A stag!" he said, mechanically notched an arrow to his bowstring, and listened.

"One rider is hard on him," he muttered, as he caught the deeper drumming of a horse's hoofs.

Then, in a flash, a big red stag bounded past him and crashed into and through a thicket at the end of the glade and was gone. The leafy bushes closed behind the hunted beast like friends. Within a space of seconds a horse carrying the King plunged up and was reined in savagely.

"Which way went the stag, boor?" shouted Rufus, his bow ready, staring about him. Then he turned his eyes impatiently to the old Bowman and recognised him.

"Thou, Outlaw! Whither went the stag?"

"I know not!"

"Liar!"

The King flung up his bow—but he was late.

Rhobart shot it from his moving hand as he lifted it.

"Clown! Thou—thou—thou art now doomed indeed . . ." mouthed the red ruffian, foaming like an epileptic. "Thou English drunkard, I have despised thee always, though I used thee! But now thou shalt die horribly! Last e'en I spared thee, believing I had hastened thee into a misjudgment of aim. I know now, from those who watched thee more shrewdly, that this was not so but, instead, deliberate, of set purpose! And now thou hast raised thy hand against the King . . ."

"The King! Thou thing, thou art no King of mine—nor thy father before thee!" said the Bowman. "Hereward went in to him—God wot possessed the Wake, not I, nor many a thousand Englishmen beside—but no oaths to him nor thee nor thine have *I* sworn. I have thee, Rufus, at the arrow's point, and nought shall avail thee, thou Norman swine!"

Far off the note of a horn came to them.

"Between the hearing of yonder horn's note and the coming of him who blew it lies the whole span of life left to thee, Rufus!" gibed the Bowman bitterly.

"Thou would'st kill thy King!" said Rufus, incredulously.

"Thou son of a Conqueror, thou art as a dead man speaking!" said the Bowman equably.

Faint and far-off rose the drumming of other hooves.

"Thou hast miscalled me many times, Rufus—English drunkard, English hog, English clown—all these and more. Thou and thy like have ever loved, above all things, to miscall the English! So it has been these many years—so it may be for a thousand years yet, but there is only one condition of English that thou—and thy like—may ever safely miscall and maltreat—and those are the English who are *dead*! . . . As thou art now!"

And the Bowman's arrow crashed through the heart of the red Norman as he pronounced it!

Not a second too soon.

Even as the body of the transfixed King sagged to the Forest floor, another arrow hummed past into the far thicket, a stag went bounding by,—and the Bowman stepped back among the trees.

He saw a horse reined in by the body, a knight he knew, one Sir Walter Tyrrell, a friend of the King, fling himself from the saddle, and stoop to peer.

He saw Tyrrell straighten up, wringing his hands, pause for a second, listening intently, then leap on to his horse, patting the creature's sweat-stained neck.

"Which? Whither?" he said hoarsely. "To Henry notifying him that he should make haste to Winchester to claim the crown—or to the coast for France!"

Tyrrell hesitated—but for a second only.

"Put not your trust in Princes," he shouted hysterically. "The coast—the coast!"—drove home his spurs and was gone—to seek sanctuary for a killing which he had not committed, but with which History would ever charge him.

The Bowman, far back in the shadows, chuckled sardonically. "They come—they go—they never learn! One Norman thinketh he hath killed another! What matter? And the Englishman goeth patiently on his way—through the shadows—as I do now!"

He moved on through the solemn, silent trees—till he emerged on to a footway almost to collide with a rubicund, grey-whiskered man leading a horse gravely overloaded with provender, wet and dry.

It was Simon the Cellarer.

"Why, Simon, old comrade! Whither goest thou?" said the Bowman.

"My old Rhobart! Whither but unto the monks at Ethelswain! Many a time and oft have they invited me to oversee, to control and to catalogue their vast and hitherto *un*catalogued cellars! Now I go . . . melancholy, thinking I should never again see thee, Bowman! Come thou with me—and aid me. They are goodly men—and well-faring."

The Bowman slipped his arm round the ancient shoulders of the old cellarer.

"All my life have I desired to become the Assistant-Cataloguer of Great Cellars hitherto uncatalogued, my Simon! Lead on!"

"Yea—but first we will explore a bottle of the King's Best! I have it here, Rhobart!"

"Where?" asked the Bowman anxiously. . . .

But, as far as Mr. Honey was concerned, the contents of that bottle of the King's Best was never savoured, for at that moment he awoke in his London flat. . . .

For a few seconds he did not know whether to be pleased or not; did not know whether he was proud of himself as he had been in that incarnation or whether he was not.

It had been almost brutally vivid—it lingered in his mind with quite extraordinary clearness.

He thought intently for a few minutes.

Then, as an Englishman, he knew. . . .

COMMENTARY

ON

THE ADVENTURE CALLED KING'S ARCHER

Hobart was quite extravagantly pleased with the adventure of the archer when I took it to him.

"Ha!" he said. "I was a very different and very much better man when I was Archer to Rufus than I was when I had poor old Jorj murdered in the days of Demetrius—murdered so that I could get his job, God forgive me. Yes, a far better man—a finer type altogether. You have portrayed me well, Bertram. Thanks, old chap. I *was* like that—a boozy grandsire, true, but I had my good points. I remember it all as if it were yesterday, now that the Lama has opened a door so long locked."

"But, honestly, could you really shoot like that?" I asked. "That trick of glancing an arrow from a pillar—isn't that just a bit far-fetched?"

Hobart shook his head.

"If you go down into the New Forest and look at that rather shabby triangular iron monument which has been fitted over the stone originally put to mark the spot where I blasted the life out of that red bully you will see inscribed thereon among other things (including one shocking grammatical error) that Rufus was killed by an arrow '*glancing* from a tree!' The man who first put up that inscription so long ago guessed who had shot Rufus—as many people must have guessed—and I see now that this was his oblique way of trying to perpetuate *my* memory. Subtle, eh? I invented that glancing shot . . . Though, as you know, I did not use it for Rufus—I took no more chances with him than I would take with some of our continental war-lords if I had them at the point of a rifle. I like your presentation of that experience enormously. . . . They were difficult days—often terrible. The aftermath of successful invasion must always be terrible."

He sighed, thinking, mentally re-living what he had already lived twice.

"You spoke of Hereward the Wake when you told me the story. Tell me, Hobart, what sort of a chap was *he*?"

But Honey shook his head.

"I can't. Once back in this life I can't remember anything that happened *before* I awoke in an earlier incarnation—nor anything that happened afterwards in that incarnation. I have often wondered what happened to my niece, Edyth, and that boy. And what happened to Simon and me. Did I stay with the monks? Was I ever in-lawed again or was I wolf's-head, as the saying went, all the rest of my life? I don't know—I shall never know."

He looked so genuinely distressed that I dropped it. Instead, I poured him a good stiff drink, passed it to him, and raised my own glass to him.

"Well, so be it," I said. "The past is past, I suppose. But, in the present, 'Here's to you, Rhobart! And to all the little Rhobarts of whom, I have no doubt, you were the papa. And to the undying fire of courage and endurance that has come down the ages within them!"

His face lit up, and we drank to that far-away old boozy English bowman with a sincerity that was as real as it was profound.

BERTRAM.

THE FIFTH PILL

TANK NUMBER ONE

MR. HONEY was not a mean man, and therefore was not prone to the practice of stinginess—so that it gave him a small shock when he first realised that it had never once occurred to him to share with any of his friends the dubious joys which he was extracting from the use of the Lama's pills. A pill that has the power to transport, temporarily, the person who swallows it back into a life which he has lived hundreds maybe thousands of years ago is, at least, a novelty and, at most, a miracle. And if a person possesses some hundreds of such miracles surely, reflected Mr. Honey, it is only bare decency to present a miracle or two to a friend.

He acted on the idea with the impulsiveness of a naturally generous man. He had very little difficulty in selecting from his numerous acquaintances three people to be recipients of his gifts. One of these was his friend the Bishop of Stretchester, a serious man who claimed to suffer from his nerves. Mr. Honey strongly recommended one of his pills, and promised the Bishop another if he found that the first pill did anything for his nerves. It did something for them—it came near to utterly wrecking them, for the Bishop "dreamed" (as he described it) that he had been changed into Balaam's ass and, as such, spent a considerable time experiencing the various vicissitudes of that ill-starred quadruped. The Bishop did not ask for another pill, and Mr. Honey did not explain that if he had once been Balaam's ass then he had evidently got on in the world.

Another pill Mr. Honey gave to a politician friend of his, but this, too, was far from proving a staggering success. The politician "dreamed" that he was a Trappist monk vowed to everlasting silence. To a politician this, naturally, was slightly worse than "dreaming" he had died and gone to hell.

The last of the three pills given away by Mr. Honey in his outburst of generosity he gave as a headache cure to an elderly Dowager Countess who admired, or said she admired, his literary work. The lady afterwards complained that the pill had made her "dream" that she was the celebrated giant Goliath at about the time Goliath met with one of the younger generation, a lad named David, the local sling champion. David did nothing to ameliorate the Dowager's headache—rather the contrary, in fact. She said that the pills did not agree with her, and shed some of her admiration for Mr. Honey's writing.

So he abandoned the practice of giving away the pills.

"These people can't take it—or the pills, either. Queer pasts they seem to have had—unless they were really *my* pasts. Probably they were. In that case I may as well enjoy—bah!—my own pasts!" he said, one evening as he sat over his port, looking at the pill-bottle.

"After all, I suppose it's a habit one has to get used to." He threw the end of his cigarette away and tilted out a pill. In a wildish kind of way he hoped that it might take him back to an incarnation in which he had been Louis the Fifteenth of France. Hope, after all, is both lawful and inexpensive—and Louis' girl-friend, Madame du Barry, had always exercised a curious fascination for him.

But, as it chanced, the du Barry did not put in an appearance that evening—Mr. Honey awoke to a somewhat sterner love affair than that of Louis XV and Madame.

He swallowed a glass of port, then the pill, then another port and lay back at his ease. At least, he thought he was lying back at his ease, but within a space of seconds he perceived himself to be mistaken—for, as his head cleared, he discovered that he was lying back against one of the hardest rocks he had ever felt. Nor was it merely hard, it was knobby, and it was veneered with ice. He noted that he was clad in an abbreviated fur shirt—far too abbreviated for comfort, for it was cold enough to crack a thermometer.

He leaped to his feet like a man on springs, took one swift glance at a pallid sun which was low in the western sky, and at a swiftish trot headed north along a rocky track. In one hand he carried a species of axe—a sharp-edged bit of chipped flint bound with sinew into the cleft end of a haft of wood. In the other hand he carried a strip of frozen meat at which he gnawed as he went. On his back he bore a skin sack.

His eyes, as he glanced continually at the sinking sun, were anxious—for he was now a dweller in the age which we know as the Paleolithic, and that was not a good age in which to spend a midwinter night outside of a cave, even in the low altitude of the plains. And Mr. Honey was not in the altitude of the plains. Far from it. He was about nine thousand feet up on the mountainside, and he had a long way to go in the very short time which remained before darkness and, as the first breath of a coming blizzard was already whispering in his chilled ears, a degree of cold capable of killing a North Pole narwhal.

Not that he was worried—but a little anxious, yes. He had made the trip before and, just as he had done to-day, he had paused after crossing the Ridge for a little sleep. But he had never before slept quite so long. Accustomed as he and his kin were to shave things pretty fine, he was not at all sure that this time he had not shaved them a little too fine.

He was gaiting along at a definitely smart clip and the bulging skin bag that hung by a strap across his shoulder was weighing a lot more heavily than it seemed to weigh when he had started from home, full-fed, a couple of days before. He halted a second to readjust it, then hurried on, slapping his horny-soled bare feet down on to the rocky track in serious earnest.

He muttered something about the bag as he went, and presently halted with his hands raised as though he intended to slip it off, leave it behind and get along in a higher gear.

But he did not do so. Instead, he laughed, rather a grim, sardonic laugh, shouted something insulting to a big condor-like bird that, overhead, was effortlessly following his course down the narrow, precipice-bordered track, in a companionable kind of way, and pushed on.

"I know of no man who ever visited the tribe of the Boughswingers without presents and lived to tell the tale," he muttered. "Nor any lover who brought away a bride from among them without first paying down the ready *shugar*[1] for her!"

He was right. The tribe of the trees from whom he was expecting shortly to collect the lady he loved (in the Paleolithic manner) were, after their primitive fashion, pretty good business men.

They knew Hob—indeed, they were unusually well acquainted with him. But they were not in the habit of trusting a man of another tribe merely because they knew him. They were very practical people—as people had to be in those far-distant days. "Fair words and hearty promises produce no flint axes" was one of their everyday proverbs. "Show us the shugar—don't word-paint it!" was another. Some of their descendants, thousands of years later, settled in Missouri . . .

Hob knew that he had to deliver his sack of goods or come away minus his bride and possibly minus a good deal of his more important anatomy as well.

So he pushed on down the track pretty cheerfully, skirting the precipices and side-stepping the slippery spots with the sureness of a mountain goat.

It was just as the lower rim of the red sun touched the jagged horizon, and Hob slowed down, crossing with great caution a ledge no more than a few inches wide which hung over a thousand feet of sheer precipice, that the huge

[1] *Shugar* was the word they used in the Paleolithic age when they meant what we mean when we say "money." Their money was not the pure, milled-edge coin nor the prettily printed paper so popular with us. It was many things—in Mr. Honey's case, in this incarnation, it consisted of about three-quarters of a hundredweight of amber, turquoise-matrix, mother of pearl shell and rough gold nuggets, designed for the more ostentatious forms of decoration.—Bertram.

bird of prey made a pass at him, and all-but got him. But Hob was expecting this, and was ready. He grabbed a lucky hand-hold and gave the bird the flint axe on its flat skull. These prehistoric gentlemen did not miss much that they aimed at. In a dim kind of way the Paleolithic condor regretted its impulsiveness for as long as it takes a condor with fatal concussion to fall a thousand feet.

Hob grinned faintly, and completed his crossing of the most dangerous part of the ledge.

The path widened very quickly now, and the downhill-going was much easier. This was just as well, for the icy dusk was now close at hand. An occasional snowflake, not larger than a smallish sea-gull, sailed silently past Hob now, increasing slowly in numbers. These flakes were no more than slight hints, but Hob knew that what they hinted at was something more like an avalanche than a snowstorm as we understand the word.

He had steamed up very nearly to his speed limit when he heard a thin sound far behind him which stopped him dead in his tracks, listening—listening body and soul.

Wolves!

He acted fast—he had to. He slipped off the bag, which went rolling over the precipice, and went forward groping in his pouch for a bit of skin and some sinews. As he ran he knotted the sinew round the fur into the form of a rough lumpy ball. Then, still running, he gashed his arm with his flint axe and soaked the skin with blood. In a few minutes he reached the spot he wanted—a place where the sheer precipice had yielded to a steep slope. He stopped, permitted himself to bleed a little on the edge of the track, smeared it about with the soaked ball and started the ball rolling irregularly down the slope. He swiftly bound a bit of skin over the wound. Then he took a mighty leap up to a rock on his left hand, and desperately struggled along the face of the rocky wall for a few dozen yards.

Then he dropped to the track again, and began to hurry in real earnest. He was accustomed to speeding—one did that from childhood upwards in those days; he knew every inch of the way; he was going downhill; he was on his way to fetch his bride; and he had a pack of wolves behind him.

He was now moving at a rate which made it difficult to see whether his feet actually touched the ground more than once in about ten yards or not. He looked as if he was on the point of "taking off" from an aerodrome—as if he might soar into the air at any moment. His ears were set back like a hare's, so that he decreased the wind resistance to that extent, and, moreover, could nicely estimate the volume of the observations of the wolf-pack behind him. These were dying down slightly—naturally enough, for in the first flush of his enthusiasm Hob could have outstripped practically anything but one of the latest models of single-seat fighters. Yet, fast as he was going, he notched up a record at the sudden clamour that outraged the air when the wolves reached the bloodstained point from which the ball of skin had started down the slope.

Then the howlings died away and came no more. They had followed the blood scent.

Half an hour later, in pitch darkness, Hob scrambled over the high stockade round the forest clearing in which the tribe of the Boughswingers had their village, shouting his name and pacific intentions very loudly indeed.

Most of the Boughswingers had gone to bed—as *they* understood the art of going to bed. It was an extremely simple business. When bedtime arrived they stopped sitting about on the chilly ground and climbed up trees. The rich crawled into little tree huts made of sticks and dried grass and reeds; the poor sat in forks and crotches; lovers did the best they could. All seemed satisfied.

As Hob landed over the stockade two hefty shadows slid down the trunk of a big beech tree at rather dizzy speed, armed with enormous stone-headed clubs or bats, and interviewed him.

"Be not alarmed, brothers. It is but Hob of the Clams come to collect his bride, the beautiful Lumpee," said Hob very swiftly, for the Boughswingers were bat-sharps of no mean order.

Recognising him, they grunted that he was lucky to have got there at all, and returned to their bedrooms up the beech.

Hob thanked them for their hearty welcome, and picked himself a tree—the one which he fancied Lumpee slept up. Evidently his fancy was wrong, or Lumpee had recently changed trees, for Hob spent the night with a tame bear-cub which the Chief of the Boughswingers was teaching to retrieve. The bear-cub was as friendly to Hob as Hob was to it, and he did not trouble to select another tree. He fitted himself into a fork, and after reflecting for a few minutes on the unromantic beginning to his expedition, fell asleep.

Next morning, after a moderate breakfast of post-dated venison, berries, roots and a nut or two, the Council of Elders, having sent the young men out to hunt game and the young women out to pick eatables off eatable-bearing bushes, sat on Hob's case.

It did not take long.

The Chief spoke first.

"You have come hither from the seashore tribe of the Clams to pay for and bear away your betrothed, Lumpee, the daughter of Humph?"

"Yes," admitted Hob.

"The price is already agreed with Humph?"

"Yes," said Hob, rather slowly.

"What says Humph?"

"Humph!" said Humph, a grim parent, who rarely said anything else.

"It is well!" said the Chief. "Produce the price, Hob."

Hob, his eyes anxiously on the smiling lady, began to explain.

"The price—yes, of course. I brought it— a good price, a noble price, a price worthy of Lumpee—I brought it away from my home. But, alas! being chased by wolves I deemed it prudent to ease my burden by depositing the sack containing the price in a safe place."

All smiles vanished.

"You have not the price?" rose a shrill, wire-drawn voice—Lumpee's.

"Well, no—yes, I have it—but not on me—not actually *with* me, so to say!"

"Humph!" said Humph.

The Chief of the Boughswingers knotted his brows, staring.

"You say that you have *not*—nay, let us be clear upon this matter. There was an agreed price for this beautiful daughter of the Boughswingers for marriage purposes? Is that correct?"

"Yes, correct, O Chief, and superbly put," admitted Hob.

"You have come now to fetch away Lumpee?"

"It is even so," said Hob.

"But you have not brought the shugar! Saying, instead, that you hid it because you were chased by a pack of wolves."

"Yes."

"For so trifling a thing—for are we not *always* being chased about by wolves? So you have the unparalleled crust to appear here demanding a wife *on credit*!"

Lumpee began to scream with anger, horror, disgust, humiliation, disappointment, mortification and a number of other emotions.

"Silence your offspring, Humph!" commanded the Chief.

Humph silenced her, and replaced his club on the ground.

"This is a very grievous affront to the Boughswingers!" stated the Chief. "Since when have outlanders believed us so low that we are willing to supply them with free wives?"

"It is an insult!" said a huge, grim-looking, muscular Boughswinger called Beetle-Brow, who was leaning on his stone-topped club, next to Lumpee, with one arm round her not unwilling waist.

The Council nodded solemnly in unison.

Hob bowed and salaamed respectfully several times. When he had finished bowing he was a good deal nearer the stockade than he had been.

The Chief seemed suddenly to lose his judicial calm.

"You come here as bold as a sabre-toothed tiger, but empty-handed, and tell us a tale like that!" he bellowed. "Evidently you conceive us to be fools. You say you were chased here by wolves! By the eternal rocks, if there were men present worth their salt you would think you were being chased hence by cave-hyenas!"

The big Boughswinger by Lumpee lurched forward—but he was slow. Hob was over the stockade and on his way like a scalded cat. He paused for a second at the top of the stockade to utter a truly blood-curdling threat.

"I go now—yea. But I will return and destroy the whole tribe of you, root and bough!" he stated shortly—and left, touching only the high spots. He may have been short of shugar but he had plenty of speed.

. . . . .

Something well over a hundred years before, Hob's great-great-great-grandfather, a famous hunter, had been trailing a huge cow-mammoth when the vast creature, by some accident or misjudgment, had got itself out on the frozen surface of a swamp[1] followed by its calf.

The frozen crust had broken, letting the mammoth through. It disappeared instantly. But the weight of the small calf made no impression on the ice, and after a wait of some hours, the baby mammoth, hungry, cold, bewildered, had fallen an easy prisoner to the patient old hunter watching it. It was fortunate for the calf that the tribe chanced at that period to be over-stocked, if possible, with food. A couple of enormous woolly rhinoceroses had fought each to a double finish just outside the village the day before, a dead whale had stranded on the beach a week before, and for miles the same beach was strewn with the carcasses of about half a million of cod which had thrown themselves out of the water, high above tidemark, in frantic flight from a school of vast cod-eating sharks that infested round about there at that period. The tribe of the Clams, therefore, was so food-ful that they could only see with difficulty, and they took no interest in the tiny mammoth. Ordinarily they would have barbecued him before he was well inside the village. Now they agreed good-humouredly with Hob's ancestor when he stated that he was going to rear the baby mammoth and bring him up as a kind of pet—use him for riding, pulling or pushing objects and so on.

Strange to relate, the ancestor had succeeded. He named the calf Lowsie, and it became greatly attached to the Hob family. For a mammoth it had a very gentle nature. In less than forty years it would follow the old

[1] Swamps and quicksands were about the only things that could kill these mammoths. They are always being dug up from such places nowadays.—Bertram.

man like a dog. It would fetch and carry for him, push rocks, pull down trees, make itself useful in many ways. For years it had slept at the old man's feet, till one night, when it was about one-third grown, it had turned over in its sleep—on to the old man's feet, and sprained both his ankles badly before he could get them out from under. After this, Lowsie slept outside. Time went on, the old man died and bequeathed Lowsie to his son, who enjoyed the mammoth's company and utilised its services for about thirty years. Then, in turn, he passed on the now fully-grown mammoth. And so it had gone on and on, generation by generation, till the mighty animal had been inherited by Hob.

Lowsie was round about a hundred and fifty years old at this period, and more than all the members of the Hob dynasty, so to express it, he had known and by whom he had been owned, he loved the present holder of the Hob title. He had grown into a fine mammoth, five tons or so, maybe a little more or slightly less,[1] and he would obey the least whisper or sign of Hob, like a trained seal. He was a grand pet, and he cost nothing—fed himself in the woods. Hob would not run from a pack of wolves if he had Lowsie with him—it was the wolves who performed the running on these occasions. Even the mighty cave-bear, or the huge, ferocious and haughty sabre-tooth tiger looked the other way, and failed to notice Hob or Lowsie when they met. Indeed, in their haughty, absent-minded way they usually climbed a tree or ducked over a precipice. Lowsie was well over twelve feet high; his gleaming white tusks were eight or nine feet long, and could have hooked an ordinary elephant of these days pretty well up to the Milky Way; his trunk was like a waterspout, and he was covered with dirt-coloured wool.

[1] Call it six ton. I am not the kind of party to grudge readers a ton of mammoth.—Bertram.

This, then, was the pet which gambolled clumsily forth to meet his beloved owner when the still furious Hob, a few days after his interview with the Boughswinger Council, came home again.

"Hello, Lowsie—good Lowsie!" said Hob, patting the vast beast somewhere just about the knee joint. It was like patting a pillar in a cathedral. Lowsie gently curled his trunk end around Hob and lifted him up on his back, where there was almost enough room to stroll about. But Hob had neither time nor inclination for idling. He told the mammoth so as they headed for the village of the Clams.

"They have insulted your Boss, Lowsie, and you have got the job of avenging him," said Hob viciously.

Lowsie wagged a tail the size of a medium bolster. Although he was probably the only really docile mammoth ever known in the history of mankind his habit of obedience, ingrained over a period of a hundred and fifty years, was greater even than his natural and acquired docility. If the Boss said, "Obliterate the Boughswingers," Lowsie was entirely willing to oblige, for he loved the Boss who, in the mammoth's low-geared mind, was the kindest, most generous Boss in the world. Quite frequently Lowsie had known him say, "Go now and get your dinner, Lowsie—eat hearty, as much and as long as you like!" The mammoth's favourite food was the tender tips of the pine boughs and there were millions of pine trees about. Probably Lowsie laboured under the delusion that these trees were Hob's personal property, and he was, in a dim-witted way, extremely grateful, or appreciative, of Hob's generosity. He was a fine specimen of a mammoth physically, but mentally his lights were a little low. Even the occasional lady mammoth he met in the vast pine forest when taking his daily snack of fifty bushels of turpentiny foliage meant very little to Lowsie for, judged by modern standards, he was sexed to about the same degree as a General Grant tank. His sex rating was somewhere round about zero on any reliable thermometer. Hence, probably, his unnatural docility. He was, of course, still very young and inexperienced—for a mammoth.

It did not take Hob very long to equip himself for the projected "mopping-up" of the avaricious Boughswingers.

He remained at home only long enough to amass a pile of dried meat, to select a spare flint axe for himself, a flint jabber or goad for Lowsie's benefit, and he was off again—lingering only to enquire whether anybody had any farewell messages for the Boughswingers.

They went a long way round to avoid the mountain tracks so that it was a week before they were within reasonable scouting distance of the stockade in the trees. Here Hob halted, gave Lowsie permission to eat for a while, and, for himself, proceeded to do a spot of Paleolithic scouting.

Shuffling silently up to the stockade, which the Boughswingers had so intelligently erected between themselves and the outside world, he paused to listen. It was dusk, and evidently the hunters had done well that day, for, judging from the volume of conversation going on within the stockade, everybody was contented with the kind of relaxed contentment which usually results from a hearty supper. A few moments' listening-in acquainted Hob with the fact that somebody had killed a large specimen of the Great Irish Elk that morning, and that everybody had eaten him that evening. They were now gossiping as they digested.

It was not long before Hob heard his own name mentioned—by the voice of Beetle-Brow, the rough who had chased him over the stockade and far beyond it.

"Yes, that was the fellow—Hob. Hob of the Clams. He came hither as bold as—as—a boulder rolling down the slope of a steep hill demanding my girl, Lumpee, as his bride. 'Very good and well,' said the Chief. 'A price was agreed for the maiden?'

" 'Yes,' said this Hob.

" 'Produce the price!' said the Chief, and believe it or not the Clam had it not—had nothing, in fact. Said so—explained he had been chased by wolves and had to throw the price into the chasm! Sounds mad—but it is true. Is it not true, Lump, old lady?"

"Absolutely," confirmed Lump, contemptuously. "He had nothing but the last year's skin he stood up in!"

"The Chief asked him if he thought the Boughswingers were in the business of supplying free wives to foreigners, and that was hint enough for me. I got my club into the 'ready' position, and Hob must have seen it, for he went over the stockade like a Stone Age kangaroo gone frantic! And that was the last seen of him. Lumpee naturally disowned him on the spot—and I got together the necessary shugar and paid the price for her then and there. So she's mine now—that so, Lump, old lady?"

"Absolutely," confirmed Lump again.

"And," resumed Beetle-Brow, "and if ever that wolf-haunted clout of a Clam comes sneaking around here again I will so deal with the front of his face that ever thereafter he shall fail to distinguish it from the back of his head!"

"For myself, I have never liked the Clams. There is something fishy about them!" said a voice.

"I ask you, what kind of a man but a Clam would expect a wife like the beautiful Lumpee *bukshee,* free gratis and for nothing!" said another voice.

"The Clams are not true men, they are a kind of salt monkey that lives in the cliff caves and eats seaweed," declared a third conversationalist.

Hob left them. He felt he had heard all he required. He found his way back to Lowsie—and his Stone Age language would have startled anything but a zero-witted mammoth.

"To-morrow at dawn, Lowsie—to-morrow at dawn!" he hissed. "Lie down, you, and keep the wind off me!"

He crept snarling into the lee of the monster, and was instantly asleep.

But he was awake at the first peep of dawn, his fury increased, rather than abated, by a good night's rest.

"You are to-day going into action for the first time, Lowsie, good mammoth, under my command. Mark that, —under my command! You will destroy the village and all within it. You will pull down all trees in which Boughswingers seek shelter and the denizens of these trees you will trample. All folk who run away you will catch and pull apart! Is that clear? Good! I will now mount!"

He mounted the huge beast like a man mounting a tank.

"Start, Lowsie!" he commanded.[1]

It was, of course, easy.

The peace-loving mammoth only required a fairly generous application of the flint goad to believe that Hob meant what he said.

He charged forward, going through the stockade as if it were cotton wool. He uprooted trees like a hungry man uprooting radishes. He shook Boughswingers out of said trees and destroyed them, as ordered by the now raving Hob. He caught fleeing Boughswingers and mowed them down. He went baresark and tried to plough up solid rock with his tusks, breaking one off and bending the other. This gave him a kind of toothache, and he became all but uncontrollable, so that, having obliterated all the Boughswingers he could see, he decided to charge a small cliff of

[1] Probably the first time a tank, or its equivalent, was used. It gave rise to the saying—now recommended to the notice of Axis leaders—"Whoso starteth things with tanks shall be finished by tanks!"—Bertram.

pure rock just outside the wood. It was quite a small cliff—probably only weighed about two hundred and seventy thousand tons. Still, it was good, close-grained rock—and it all-but concertinæd the murderous mammoth. It stretched him flat. If Hob had not slid down over his tail just in time it would have concussed him crazy.

When, presently, Lowsie returned to consciousness he was much less baresark. He felt ill and bilious and sulky. Nothing but a lifelong habit of obedience would have forced him so mechanically to respond to a screamed order by Hob to pursue two figures which were moving towards the horizon at a truly remarkable speed—the figures of Lumpee and Beetle-Brow.

Wearily, the rock-stricken, granite-drunk tank rolled after them.

Even in his lowest gear it only took the mammoth a minute or two to catch them. They parted, and ran wide of each other as the thundering monster's snaky trunk reached for them. It was the man that Lowsie grabbed, threw down and trampled.

Hob turned to shout to the staring and horrified girl.

"Ho, Lumpee! Said I not that I would return and render extinct all the tribe of Boughswingers! Wait there for me—wait . . ."

He broke off as Lowsie gave a very unusual lurch, and the south-west corner of him sank suddenly. Hob saw at once what had happened. Lowsie had caught the fugitives at the wrong spot and trampled Beetle-Brow just a trifle too enthusiastically.

They were on a frozen quicksand, and the ponderously pounding feet and great weight of the mammoth had broken the icy crust.

With a furious trumpeting Lowsie exerted his full colossal strength and tore his leg free—only to sink another leg deeper still. Then both forelegs went through.

The mammoth was doomed—he was sinking fast.

Hob glared round him, measuring the area of jagged cakes of broken ice across which he must jump to the safety of the firm ice when Lowsie sank deep enough.

A flint-headed spear went whizzing past his head. The girl Lumpee was out to avenge her people. She ran round the wreckage to recover the weapon, screaming a few of the things she intended to do to Hob if and when he leaped from the sinking Lowsie. But she was wasting her breath.

Hob saw two husky survivors from the village, their spears and axes ready, racing up. They had seen Tank No. One's disaster from their hiding places. Then, even as he realised that he was doomed, the fore-front of the mammoth sank several feet, so that it was from a steeply sloping platform that Hob desperately jumped—practically straight into the curled end of the huge flailing trunk. The mammoth clung to Hob like a forlorn hope—which he was.

Then suddenly the mammoth roared and went under, taking Hob with him. At least he would have gone the whole distance with Lowsie if at that moment he had not returned to this life and these days in the apartment of Mr. Hobart Honey.

Outside a motor bus in need of workshop attention was roaring down the street like—like a mammoth or a tank . . .

Mr. H. took two large glasses of port in quick succession. Then he said "Hah!" and poured a third. He drank it slowly, eyeing the bottle of pills with something like disgust. But his disgust, after all, was premature. He had a glorious surprise coming to him before long—out of that same bottle. As will be seen.

COMMENTARY

ON

THE ADVENTURE CALLED TANK NUMBER ONE

Hobart Honey did not appear greatly enraptured to receive my account of this incarnation. It may have been that he considered he had hung sufficient garlands around my neck for the time being or, equally, it may have been that he has always seemed to me to be quite oddly uninterested in the Stone Age. I shrugged my shoulders, lit a cigarette and said, "Well, at least read the thing before you criticise it, my dear man. After all, you are not a professional critic. And I maintain that even those chaps do occasionally take a quick glance at some of the books they review. One has to be fair."

It was as gratifying as unexpected to hear him chuckling as he read the typescript, keeping up a muttered commentary throughout.

"Yes, it was like that along the Pass across the mountains . . . terrible place. . . . Good trick that, to throw wolves off the scent. I was the first man in the world to think of that. Not bad for a Clam. . . . Humph, perfectly true about the retrieving bear—good retriever, but a damned uncomfortable bedmate. . . . Lumpee wasn't up to much, really . . . neither, for that matter, was I. Lowsie was the only really decent, honest creature in the affair. Waste of a good mammoth, really. . . . Not a pin to choose between the Boughswingers and the Clams. . . . Wretched lot. . . . 'Salt monkey,' haha! Now, where the devil did you dig up that idea? What an expression! And yet—in a way—that's about what we Clams were—a kind of salt monkey! Haha! . . . Poor lot! . . . Yes, yes, that's very like the real thing, very. . . . Lowsie was mad

—quite mad—to charge that cliff. . . . Not so mad as I was to use him for that wholesale slaughter. Running amok. . . . He would have been ruined, in any case. Yes, the quicksand was the only place for him . . . and for me, too!"

He put down the typescript, and stared at me.

"You are a competent old ass, after your fashion, you know. You've contrived to create a sort of illusion of the right atmosphere, and you certainly convey a working idea that there was a queer humour in it all. . . . I suppose you're right—it was what I asked you to do—though at the time I was a Clam we had only the merest vestiges of a sense of humour—and a pretty low one at that. Still, that wasn't your fault. Shall we have a drink?"

"Yes, we shall," I said.

BERTRAM.

THE SIXTH PILL

GARDEN OF EDEN

HIS rapidly increasing experience of the staggering possibilities of the Lama's pills had led Mr. Hobart Honey to the conclusion that the chances of any one pill landing him back into an incarnation in which he really had been a great man were not so good.

He was not proud of this—but, against that, he was getting out of the habit of being ashamed of it. As he put it to himself one evening:

"After all, I believe I've got a right to consider myself an averagely decent, civilised sort of citizen in this life, so why worry about what sort of person I was in a life I lived a few hundred or, for that matter, a few thousand years ago. Nothing can be done about it, anyway. It appears that I was the man who shot King Rufus in the year 1100. All right. What are they going to do about it? It seems that I was the eunuch that embezzled a few dozen of the wives of Prince Demetrius and sold 'em to Ptolemy, King of Egypt. Well, what if I did? They can't arrest me for it —303 B.C. was a long time ago—and the Prehistoric considerably longer. And the experiences were interesting—well worth reliving. I think I'll take another trip into the Bygone this evening!"

He settled himself comfortably in his easy chair and fortifying himself with a glass or two of wine swallowed one of the pills with practised ease.

It took him back to an incarnation in which he was an elderly carrion-eating condor who spent the whole time between rare feasts of carrion in circling round and around somewhere up in the stratosphere over the Andes reflecting on modern carrion, its scarcity and poor quality compared with the carrion of his youth.

A dull life, and of no value to an author of the twentieth century like Mr. Honey—unless a precise knowledge of what it feels like to be one of the world's leading epicures of carrion is valuable.

An evening wasted as far as Mr. Honey was concerned.

He shrugged his shoulders, took a little more wine and selected another pill.

He was conscious of a curious feeling, as the little pellet passed his glottis, that there was Something Coming this time—that he was bound for a life in which he was going to meet Folks that really were Folks. He had often enough had this feeling before, but never quite so pronouncedly. Even as he blacked out he was muttering to himself about it. . . .

He woke slowly, and, as was usual, a little confused,—with the familiar confusion of feeling that he was really

Hobart Honey, of London, but knowing that he was by no means so; feeling that he had only left London a few seconds before, yet knowing that the first foundation stone of London would not be laid for a good many years to come—that the site of London, in fact, still lay a few miles under the sea.

He felt himself cautiously, before he opened his eyes, and found himself to be highly hairy all over.

Then he scratched himself a little, and felt all the more comfortable for it.

For a few minutes he lay, pleasantly warm under the sun, breathing deeply the marvellous scents of what could only be a miraculous wealth of flowers. He listened dreamily to the soft sigh of perfumed zephyrs wandering around and about, and he knew that life was very good indeed. He scratched himself a little more, and was distantly conscious of a faint unease, which he characterised as the merest hint of hunger. Still, for a little, he lay blandly relaxed, listening to a melody of birds singing softly in the perfumed and spicy little winds about him.

At last he realised where and what he was. He was Nn the Near-Man—that is to say, the nearest creature to Man that a creature could possibly be without actually being Man himself.

He was the personal servant of the First Man of His Period—or, for that matter, of any other Period either.

Nn was very proud of this. He lay there, lost in his delicious languor like a man in a bath of warm, perfumed oil. He knew it was well past dawn, but he knew there was no need to hurry. His parrot, roosting in the fig tree under which Nn had slept, would tell him when the Boss was on the point of waking up.

And even then, life would be as lovely. There would be no complications. Breakfast was ready. By the side of the Boss were heaps of everything good—he only had to reach out his hand—needn't even open his eyes—just only reach out and take what he touched—shaddocks, mango, durians, dates, persimmons, peaches, pomegranates, pears, grapes, plums, nectarines, oranges, figs, fruit, in fact. Fruit of every known variety and dozens of varieties not now known nor ever likely to be. And nuts—more kinds of nuts than the modern mind ever conceived—nuts that tasted like everything, from a coconut to a ham sandwich or a chocolate sundae.

For this was the Garden of Eden, and Nn's boss was Adam. . . .

He lay there dreamily, thinking of this truly noble First Man whom he was privileged to serve and to adore; and of the old days, when he had left the wandering tribe of Near-men, to which he belonged, to journey on through the tree-tops in which they spent roughly ninety-five per cent of their valueless time—wisely, for the country was unlimited of lions and teemed with tigers and similar meat-eating creatures.

"How fortunate I was," mused Nn, "to have been found by him when I was!"

That was entirely true, for Nn was in somewhat of a jam when he first set eyes on Adam.

He had come down out of the tree-tops, at the edge of the forest where it joined the desert, to get a drink of water at a pool surrounded by tall rocks. He stepped round the tallest rock and found that he was not the only denizen of the district who liked a little water now and then. Eleven maneless lions, six tigers, quite a number of leopards, several black panthers, four rhinoceroses, six bull elephants, nine cow ones, and about a couple of dozen big buffaloes were around the pool also.

Nn took a look at them all and turned a double backward somersault—into the rock, due to a sort of over-anxiety, very natural in one so solitary and unarmed.

They, in their turn, took a look at the Near-Man. He was one of these scrawny, scraggy Near-Men and quite a few of the menagerie were uninterested in him. But not all of them—six lions, three tigers, most of the leopards and all the black panthers started for him, and he had already said farewell to his native tree-tops when, suddenly, there strolled round another rock a being whose appearance on the scene short-circuited *all* local activities like a flash of lightning.

All the animals rose, politely, and those that were bounding towards the Near-Man suddenly ceased bounding. They slewed round, trying sheepishly to look as if they had only been hurrying to the Near-Man to gambol with him a little.

They wagged their tails apologetically, then placed them between their legs, as they stared past—not *into* the eyes—of the new-comer, who shook his head, then laughed quietly and spoke briefly. Evidently it was a word of friendly advice to go while going was possible, for they went like guilty things glad of a chance to go. The elephants, rhinoceroses and buffaloes did not go, but stood about in attitudes of respect and deference.

Yet the superb new-comer, noted the Near-Man, was not merely unarmed—he was undressed—well, nude. It was something in his eyes that quelled the animals—Nn took a look in the eyes and felt quelled himself—quelled but adoring. He was still quaking from the shock of the great beasts, and as he stared dumbly at the magnificent apparition who had saved him he trembled from some other cause that was not fear. Gratitude—admiration—something of that sort, no doubt.

He saw a tall creature—like a god, he would have thought, if he had ever heard of a god—immensely tall, almost gigantic by modern standards, but symmetrical to the last decimal of an inch. Under his golden skin, smooth muscle rippled and played at every movement; under a close helmet of crisply-curled gold hair, and a broad, smooth brow, shone, with an electric intensity a pair of blue eyes that—by the Near-Man, at any rate—could not long be looked into. The head was noble—set high on a muscular neck that was as graceful, swift and flexible as that of a cobra. On the clean, clear, curved lips was the friendliest smile that the Near-Man had ever known or dreamed of—and over all the glowing strength and beauty, and in spite of the unbearable brilliance of those piercing eyes, there was, the Near-Man sensed, a monumental and virginal innocence.

Nn suddenly bowed down, his face in the sand, trembling. . . . He did not know it yet, but he had been looking at Man—at Adam, the First Man—and he was not accustomed to that sort of thing. The Founder of the race of Man was, rather obviously, something special—well, look at *us*! . . .

A golden voice, strong as sunlight, gentle as dusk, came to the Near-Man as he abased himself.

"Be not afraid!"

Then, as he quaked, hiding his face in the hot sands, the trembling Near-Man felt an arm, strong as steel, yet gentle as compassion, pass round him.

"Why, thou poor thing, be not afraid, I say. Thou art with *me*, and henceforward thou shalt be under my protection—and I am *Man*!"

He lifted the scrawny wretch, like a rag, from the sand.

"Courage!" he said, and looked at Nn with smiling, brilliant eyes.

"Art thou hungry? Nay? Art thou thirsty? Yea, I see—thou camest here for that? Drink, then, and come with me."

"Yes, sir!" said Nn the Near-Man humbly.

He had drunk his fill while Adam waited. Then they had turned their backs on the pool and strolled together across the desert to the Garden of Eden—having established, though, in their innocence, neither knew it, the first social distinction known on earth. . . .

It was upon this event that Nn pondered dreamily as he lay, still half-asleep, that morning. He smiled—a trick he had learned from Adam—as he remembered it all.

Then a small cloud passed over the sun of his personal content as he remembered something else. They had been happy enough, he and his master, for months after he had secured the situation. But it had been a sinecure, judged by modern standards. That is to say, one cannot be a valet to a gentleman who does not wear clothes, nor can one be a cook to an employer who lives on an exclusive diet of fruit and nuts. One can, of course, crack his nuts for him, but why painfully crack nuts between two rocks for an easy Hercules who can crack his own between finger and thumb?

No—Nn was not overworked.

Perhaps that was why he became so observant of Adam.

Latterly he had begun to suspect that Adam was bored and lonely. He, Nn, thought of the word as "lonely," though he hardly knew what it meant. But he knew this, that the manner of his master was more and more frequently distrait; that he turned at eventide away from his lookings, his expectancies, as if he were sad and, in a vital way, distressed. . . .

Then, one morning, Nn's parrot, Irony (so called because Nn thought it was a pretty sound), a beautiful sketch in scarlet, green, gold, blue and pale pink, which had been nattering to itself for a long time—rather like a well-satisfied person talking in its sleep—uttered a sudden ear-piercing whistle.

It was, as both Nn and Irony—the only living thing after Adam, Nn loved—understood it, an alarm.

Nn woke suddenly as the bird, abandoning the alarm, began to talk.

"Somebody hath come here in the night! Nn—somebody hath come in the night!"

Nn sat up.

"It is well," he said. "I will see to it. Meantime, wake not the Chief with thy whistlings! Where is the person who hath come in the night? Quietly!"

Nn got up.

"Show me," he commanded.

"This way," said the parrot.

Nn followed a flutter of scarlet wings. . . .

She was lying, fast asleep, under a fig tree not far from Adam.

Nn took a look, caught his breath, and decided, without any difficulty at all, that he had never seen anything remotely resembling it in his life.

Beauty? Why, she dimmed the sunrise!

Nn stared—beauty-stricken.

Irony fluttered down to perch on his shoulder, took a long, long look, and screwed its gaudy neck to look up at Nn.

"Hast thou ever observed the like in the whole period of thy natural life?" it asked.

"Nay, bird, not so. I have not seen," muttered Nn. "It dimmeth mine eyes!"

He spoke the bare truth. The little, deep-sunken eyes of the Near-Man were full of inexplicable tears.

"She is lovely past understanding," said the parrot.

"Why dost thou say *she*?" asked Nn, puzzled. "She? She? That is a word I have not heard!"

The parrot chuckled—much as present-day parrots chuckle.

"I invented it! I, the parrot! It is a good word and it will frequently be heard when the world grows older."

"I think so, too!" said Nn. Still staring through his unconscious tears, he continued. "Bird, thou art wise, well experienced and far-travelled! Thinkest thou that She will permit such as I to serve her, to attend her, to follow humbly in her shadow, ever-obedient, ever-attentive to her least wish?"

"Yea—and even so," said Irony. "She will permit! Thou shalt never lack somewhat to perform in her service, Nn! As I believe it to be!"

He fluttered a scarlet wing and scratched a purple poll.

"She is the first thing of any importance to take place in the history of the Garden," he said. "And I, the parrot, Irony, the wise bird, advise thee that thou shouldest notify the Boss without loss of time!"

"Yes, that will I!" said Nn—and lingered still. "I mind me now how he hath gazed so wistfully down the vistas! Thinkest thou, bird, that he hath gazed for such as She?"

"I am incurably convinced of it," said the parrot. "How could it be otherwise? Look at her!"

Nn looked some more. He had been looking all the time they had been talking, but his eyes were not weary.

Yet he dared not linger.

"Watch well over She while She still sleeps!" he said. "I will now notify the Boss!"

He crept away, looking over his shoulder. He flattened an ear against a coconut palm as he walked sideways and so, abruptly, looked to his front . . .

Adam was awake, eating fruit.

He smiled on Nn as the Near-Man crept up.

"Sir," said Nn, a little hysterically, "*She* hath arrived in the night!"

Adam bounded to his feet, like a deer.

"*She?* . . . That is a word which I have not heard!" he said.

"Yet it will never again be unknown—said the parrot, sir!" said Nn, inventing boldly, though he was abasing himself to the ground.

"Thou art strangely humble, Nn!" observed Adam.

"Sir, I have seen that to render me humble!" said Nn—which was pretty fair for a Near-Man.

"Take me there," said Adam, smiling, "and let us see if it can humble *me*!"

So Nn took him—and left him there.

Even if he had looked over his shoulder—as he did—Nn would have seen no more than a superb example of Love at First Sight. . . .

To say that Eve was the loveliest woman Adam had ever seen would, of course, be equivalent to saying precisely nothing. He had never seen a woman before. (There were, he understood, a number of near-women, relatives of Nn, haunting about in the tree-tops of the forests, but these he classed, rightly, with the orangs and chimps.) Eve was something new—too new to be true. For a full hour he gazed upon her, thrilled and fascinated.

"She is utterly beautiful, yet She is different from me. She is round in places where I am flat. Yet I am beautiful, too!" he said, naïvely but quite truthfully. "So I suppose flat is beautiful and round is also beautiful. How nice. I wonder if she would mind if I touch her—it would be wonderful to touch her. And, after all, she is mine—everything in the garden is mine. It must be. Besides, it cannot be intended that I should stand here and stare at her for ever. She cannot have come here just to be stared at in her sleep. She must have been sent into the world for some good purpose, though what on earth I am going to do with her I do not know. Perhaps *she* would know—I will awaken her and see."

Some dim instinct checked his outstretched hand—a faint, far consciousness that perhaps it would be just as well to *provide* something for her before he woke her—a little breakfast, a selection of mixed fruit or something of that sort. He thought hard. Yes, definitely the tactful, propitiating thing to do, he decided.

It was an important decision—probably the most important decision ever made in the world—for it started a fashion which has persisted to this day—if that instinct to propitiate and please womenkind which is inextricably a part of mankind's make-up can properly be called a fashion.

He arranged the fruit as attractively as he could within easy reach, then very gently smoothed her cheek with the backs of his curved fingers.

"O, lovely one!" he whispered. "Wilt thou not wake up now, please?"

Her eyes opened so instantly that—as it occurred to Adam long afterwards—she might almost have been already awake. For a long time the deep amethyst eyes countered the electric gaze of Adam—then, surprisingly, they fell. For a few seconds only.

Then she raised a slim hand to hold Adam's, still caressing her cheek.

"Oh—oh—oh—but I have dreamed of thee this whole night long," she said in a voice so magic and so musical that Adam thrilled like a plucked harp-string.

"Sayest thou so, O Splendour of the Dawn!" replied Adam, trembling. "And I have sought throughout Eden and far across the deserts beyond it these many days and desperately dreamed these many nights for what it was I knew not, but which I know now is that which I have found. It was for thee I looked and longed!"

They stared at each other. Again her eyes fell.

"Mine eyes are dazzled," she cooed.

"But mine are enriched!" said Adam, and took her in his arms.

"But nay—nay! It is so public here!" she demurred.

"Not so," said Adam. "This is private property—private as far as the eye can reach, and beyond and beyond that again."

"But whose?" murmured Eve.

"Mine! Save only for one small, gnarled and writhen tree!"

Eve took him in her arms.

"Ours," she sighed.

"Nay, *thine*!" said Adam, generous as he was beautiful. "With this—all this—forever I endow thee—for thy sweet beauty's sake!"

That, too, in its way, was another important decision.

She kissed him, murmuring and fond. . . .

This, being the record of Mr. Hobart Honey's experience in the incarnation of Nn the Near-Man, is not the proper place in which to follow in any sort of detail the lovely life of Adam and Eve during their first few months in the Garden of Eden.[1]

Probably the most beautiful, possibly the noblest, certainly the first Love Story in the world, it went, in its superior way, pretty well like all subsequent genuine love affairs. It had its ups and downs, of course,—and Nn was mainly concerned with its downs. Few lovers require the attendance of either a Near-Man or a parrot when their affairs are going well, so Nn and his parrot were thrown pretty much on their own resources for a long time after the arrival of Eve.

[1] Should any frenzied Public Demand for such a record of Life in the Garden of Eden arise, no doubt it can be furnished upon receipt of the usual fees by . . . Bertram.

They managed.

Then, one day, Nn, strolling about the Garden with nothing to do, paused in surprise before the tree which Adam had always firmly instructed him was not, in any circumstances whatever, to be touched.

"Nor, mark ye well, Nn, is fruit to be plucked from it—never—in no circumstances whatever," Adam adjured him.

"No, sir!" he had promised, never believing that such an ugly, gnarled, knotty, twisted, inexplicable-looking tree would ever bear any fruit.

Now, to his amazement, the tree was brilliant with the most exquisitely-shaped and coloured fruit the Near-Man had ever seen—and he had seen considerable fruit in his time.

He hung about for a while, admiring it. Naturally, it never occurred to him to touch it after Adam's prohibition. But it was otherwise with Irony, the parrot, which flew across before Nn could forbid it, and tried the fruit.

"It's good—of its kind," said the bird. "It kind of stimulates your mind—though, for flavour, I prefer a good pomegranate!"

Nn, startled at the freedom of the rainbow-hued bird on his shoulder, was about to move on when a being moved out from behind the twisted trunk of the tree—a tall, dark, handsome brute in man's shape who would have reminded Nn of Mephistopheles if he had ever heard of Mephistopheles.

This one had fixed the startled Near-Man with a pair of glittering eyes.

"Leave those apples alone!" he commanded.

"Yes, sir," said Nn hurriedly, shuddering under the glare of those mesmeric eyes.

"Return whence thou camest and tell the Lady of Eden—that lovely Human called by the First Man Eve, that the fruit of the tree has ripened and is ready. Tell her no more—nor less—than I have said."

"Yes, sir," said Nn, humbly. "What name shall I say, sir?"

"Name? Name?"

The Dark One smoothed his gleaming, pointed beard, reflectively.

"Name? Say The Snake"—his eye fell on a patch of tall, gently wind-waved grass beyond the Tree—"say The Snake-in-the-Grass sent word."

He laughed. It was a silently suggestive sound, like the flicker of forked lightning seen afar off.

"No. Say A. Snake, Esq. sent word. She will know! Mention it not to Adam! Dost thou understand?"

The Near-Man hung fire.

"Sir," he quavered, "to my Lord Adam, who saved me from the great beasts, I mention all things."

"Fool," said the parrot, who had partaken of the fruit.

"Well said, bird or evil spirit, I know not—nor care," said Snake. "Mark it well, Near-Man, that if the Lady of Eden thinks it fitting that her Lord should know then *she* will tell him—not such as *thou* art, Near-Man."

"Yes, sir—no, sir," said Nn.

"Get gone!" said Snake, dangerously.

Nn got went. . . .[1]

Her laugh, when Nn passed on his message, sounded as innocent and as charming as the laugh of a child about to engage upon a trifling mischief.

And, indeed, it was no more to her than a trifling mischief. She had only once deceived Adam before—that time when he was calling her and it had seemed to her to be just a playful little amusing thing to hide behind some bushes as if she were far away. She had come out at once

[1] Origin of the word "slunk." When we say a person "slunk"—we mean he "got went away hurriedly" . . . In a way.—Bertram.

when he sounded forlorn and frightened. They had cried a little about that—it was a new thing—but in the end they had laughed.[1]

Nn did as he was told next morning when Adam had gone, for once alone, to bathe.

"Yes—I understand," said Eve, distantly. Later, lurking in the brushwood, Nn saw her pick up a woven basket and go out in the direction of the forbidden tree.

"Oh, she is wrong!" lamented Nn, in a dumb, instinctive way.

"Fool, she is utterly right," said the parrot—not so polite as formerly. The fruit of the Tree of Knowledge was toughening its psychology—if any.

"I must follow her and report to the Lord Adam," said Nn.

"You must mind your own business!" said the parrot, acidly. "That's common sense—if not more."

"You're telling me," said Nn, "what, I suppose, I ought to know for myself—only I don't! Yet, I know, somehow I feel it in my spirit, she will return a different woman."

The parrot chuckled.

"This time you're telling me," said the bird cryptically. "Madam is not a one to stand still and congeal. Madam is a lady who progresses fast!"

"Why do you call her 'Madam'? That is a new word," said Nn.

"And a good one! It is a word which will endure in no uncertain fashion for All Time, brother!" prophesied the sagacious bird—correctly. . . .

. . . . .

[1]The birth of a new joke was always difficult and painful. Hiding from your husband is an old joke nowadays. Eve first thought of it.—Bertram.

She came back, flushed, excited, and too lovely to be true. In her hand she carried a little basket of fruit.

Even Adam, getting a little more used to her than he had once been, noticed the change.

"O, Glory of The Garden, what hath come unto thee this day? Thine eyes are stars—thou art all my dreams come utterly true."

He slipped his arm around her.

But Eve only laughed.

"I have had an adventure. Come, eat the fruit which I have gathered for thee, and I will tell thee as thou eatest!"

Hungry from his swim, and attracted by the fruit, Adam did as he was told. He was halfway through the basketful by the time A. Snake, Esq., was first mentioned. Then Eve told him all he wanted to hear—and more—about the dark, handsome stranger with the queer name who had so unexpectedly come into her life.

"He was a very interesting man—though of course compared with thee he was but as a remote star is to the sun! Oh yes, I met him quite by chance—though Nn first told me of him—and he gave me this new fruit. Dost thou like it, dear heart?"

Adam reflected.

"In a way it is good, but only—in a way. Darling, it is bitter-sweet on my tongue, and my senses swim as though of some strange poison I have eaten."

He shook his beautiful head, passing his hand across his eyes.

"I have not felt like this before," he said—naturally enough, for he had eaten heartily of the Fruit of the Tree of Knowledge—and that is a strange and sharp and heady fruit.

"Moreover, Light of Mine Eyes, I like not the sound of thy new playmate, Snake!"—here Eve saw the first frown ever frowned in the history of life on his brow—"and it is in my mind that I will make a great club of hard wood and go forth and beat the life out of him ere ever this day's sun shall set. I am full of foreboding."

Somebody chuckled behind them—but it was only the parrot.

Eve's glorious eyes were round and startled.

"Adam! To beat the life out of him!" she said, shocked. "Darest thou talk so! Thou—*thou*—so gentle! Thou who hast ever loved and befriended all things—from the great beasts of the desert to the tiny humming birds that flit like jewels . . ."

She began to cry.

"Nay, nay, Dear Heart, do not weep. It was but a swift, passing anger. . . ."

"Anger! What is anger?—that is a word I have not known . . ."

"It will be heard again," said Adam dryly. "And other words that have but newly come crowding into my mind. Anger! Hate! Suspicion! Envy! Greed! Famine! Pestilence! And *War*!"

"I do not know those words—nor what they mean!" Eve was crying bitterly now.

"War! Separation! Heartbreak! *Aie!* Darling, they swarm about me like evil, stinging things. Yet shall we be always together in our hearts . . ." He broke off, staring at the fruit, struck by a new thought.

"Whence came this fruit? Came it from a gnarled and malignly-shaped, twisted and ugly tree?"

Eve nodded.

"That was the Forbidden Tree—of Knowledge. That is why I have become aware of all those new and bitter words! And of these bitter forebodings. We shall be sent forth from the Garden!"

He seized her and held her with both hands.

"Look into mine eyes, Eve!" he said urgently. "Thou! Hast thou, too, eaten of the fruit?"

She shook her head.

"I saved them all for thee, I love thee so!" she said.

But she was quick-witted. Before Adam could move, she snatched a handful of the fruit and crammed it into her mouth, and stood up at her full height with her arms flung wide.

Adam gaped as he stared, and another new word for his wife came into his mind.

"Perfection!"

"Now she, too, hath sinned and must suffer with me. Yet she remaineth most perfect in mine eyes!"

And, indeed, she was.

"Now I, too, have eaten of this bitter-sweet fruit, my Lord!" she cried. "And whatsoever it hath done unto thee so, too, let it do unto me! Together and alike we have dwelt in this Paradise—together and alike for good or ill we cleave and cling each to each, forever—and wheresoever!"

Nn, watching from a highly respectful distance, saw that the times were changing fast. He, of course, was only a Near-Man, and so knew all about that dull, grey feeling we call Misery. He was using a good deal of Misery just then.

He sat there anxiously watching the noble creatures he adored, and his spirits rose as he saw that Eve had stopped crying and, within Adam's arm, was smiling up at him as, unconsciously, they moved in the same direction as that in which went two huge, misty Forms which just then silently passed them all.

They carried between them, these gigantic Forms, a huge notice board upon which appeared, in enormous, quite unmistakable letters, the following words—

TO THE EXIT

Slowly, reluctantly, Nn—who knew something about the Outside World—rose from his scrawny haunches to follow them. Near-Man though he was, he—like his employers—could take a hint when he got one—in thirty-six-inch letters. He heard the whistle and fluster of the parrot coming up fast behind him.

"No hurry—no hurry! Why hustle things this way!" said the parrot. "We're leaving an awful lot of good fruit behind! After all, if it's Knowledge we need why not clear the tree while we are at it? May as well hang for a bushel as a peck!"

He took another large peck.

But nobody paid any attention to him! . . .

Adam and Eve hesitated for just a moment—looking a while wistfully back at a very lovely scene. . . .

"Lord, ain't they a beautiful couple?" said the parrot, impulsively. "They will always be looking back like this—these couples! Come on, Nn!"

Near the Exit Adam and Eve checked again, looking out to the arid and rocky desert.

"Oh, how harsh and terrible!" cried Eve.

Adam laughed low.

"It might be worse! Come, Dear Heart!"

Only Nn, scuffling along behind them, heard her answer.

"With thee—*anywhere*!"

The parrot hung over them all, working its wings like a kind of mill.

Suddenly it squawked.

"There he is behind the banyan—seeing us off! Sir! If thou dost really desire to club him now is the time!"

"Not that it would do any good!" muttered the uncanny fowl to itself. "This is the work of a gang, if I miss not my guess!"

Adam and Eve looked back. The creature calling himself A. Snake, Esq., was, as the parrot said, watching them from behind a big banyan tree. But even as Adam flushed and started for him, Snake vanished before their eyes.

Eve caught Adam's hand, and they turned again to the Exit, towards which the Forms were impatiently and peremptorily beckoning them.

"Place is full of strangers and illusionists," muttered the parrot.

"Art thou coming, Nn?" called Adam.

"Yes, sir!" said Nn, humbly, hurrying up.

Adam looked up, his blue eyes gleaming.

"And thou?" he asked the parrot.

"Sir," said the gaudy one, "thou can'st never make the grade without me—for I am what the new words will some day call a Sense of Humour!"

Adam laughed.

"So be it," he said.

His arm tightened around Eve.

"Come, then," he said. "Let's face it!"

But, of them all, it was only Nn who did not face it—for it was at the very moment that they all went forward into the desert that he awoke in his London flat, once more Mr. Hobart Honey.

He sat a long time quite still, thinking very deeply. He was not proud that this sample of the Lama's pills had shown him personally as only a Near-Man—but, against the debit of that he could set the credit of having been the personal servant of the unique specimen of mankind that, rather obviously, Adam was.

And yet, after a while, it was upon Eve that his mind closed most tenderly—Eve, Mother of All . . .

He reached for a large glass of port with a pang of regret that the power of the pill had waned so soon. He would have liked to have been in the forefront of the Battle of Life just a bit longer. That they had won it was, of course, obvious—the fact that he, Hobart Honey (not to mention a world-ful of other descendants), existed proved that.

COMMENTARY
ON
THE ADVENTURE CALLED GARDEN OF EDEN

Judging from the various expressions that flitted over his face, Hobart read my account of his experience in Eden with mixed feelings. He laughed a good deal, and several times I thought he was going to cry. He muttered considerably, as he read.

"A minor *rôle* . . . as usual," he said discontentedly at the beginning. "Not Bertram's fault, that, at any rate."

Presently he drew in his breath so sharply that I looked up.

"What's wrong?" I asked.

"Eh? Oh, yes—it all came back to me so poignantly when Adam rescued me from the beasts!" He quoted Adam's observation as if it were a new thing to me.

" 'Why, thou poor thing, be not afraid, I say. Thou art with me, and henceforward thou shalt be under my protection—and I am *Man*!' You'll never know—nobody in the world can ever know—how that sounded to me at that moment. A few seconds before I had been looking into the eyes of the mán-eaters, and then I felt *his* arm round me. *Me*—fresh from the trees—hardly fit for Near-Man-eaters to devour . . ."

He broke off, lost in his reading.

Presently he nodded, chuckling.

"What a bird, what a bird! There never was a parrot to compare with Irony—we were like close relatives, Irony and I. He was good for us all. . . . Yes, yes. '*Come then, —let's face it!*' Yes, Adam said that, his arm close round her, looking out at the desert with the eyes of a Conqueror! . . . Yes, you brought it back to me, my dear Bertram!"

He stared at me for some moments, rather as if he thought I was some new variety of beetle or something of that kind.

"You're a queer kind of writer," he said. "Sometimes it's as if a clown were writing the account, sometimes it's as if a woman were writing it, sometimes it's as if a racketeer or gangster were writing it, and sometimes it might be the work of a half-daft minor poet or an impudent child!"

"Thanks," I said, shortly. "It was written to *your* specification, my dear Hobart!"

He stared.

"I didn't mean that in an entirely uncomplimentary sense, you know," he said, and turned to the sideboard.

"A drink, don't you think?" he suggested.

"Yes, I think."

BERTRAM.

THE ELEVENTH PILL

ABBOT'S ENVOY

ALTHOUGH Mr. Honey would not have described himself as a vain or conceited man (for he did not secretly consider himself to be *more* than about eighty per cent superior to the person called variously The Man in the Street, John Citizen, or The Average Man) he still was finding it difficult to relinquish the preposterous notion that the Lama's pills would occasionally re-establish him in the ancient glories which, he felt, must once have been his in one of the lives in which he had been Somebody of Importance.

So far it had not worked out like that.

This had distressed him a little at first, but he was now getting hardened to it—and he was greatly gratified to come to the pleasing conclusion that his experiences were producing a marked hardening of his present-day character, a great development of his personality, and a startling addition of steeliness to his outlook on life. He had noticed that these days he was getting better attention from head waiters and much better servility from under waiters; that people listened when he spoke instead of speaking while he listened; that large numbers of folk said "Yes, Mr. Honey," instead of "I totally disagree with you!" He had noticed that girls seemed to look back at him over their shoulders more while he looked back over his shoulder at them less.[1]

Little indications like that . . .

"Not so bad—it might be worse," he concluded one evening, and picked up the pill-bottle. "Could be better! Still, let us try that large one."

He shook out a pill and washed it down with his customary glass of port.

In five seconds he looked, where he sat, exactly like a middle-aged author sound asleep—but that was far from being entirely correct.

He woke, or seemed to wake, to the sound of wind hooting on a deep note through a large keyhole, but almost immediately he became aware that the droning sound was the voice of a man addressing some person called "Tuck."

Still a little hazy, as usual he sat for a minute or so with closed eyes, getting his bearings. He did not feel

[1] How he discovered this without looking back at them is difficult to explain. All explanations, therefore, must be regretfully sidestepped.—Bertram.

himself to be eavesdropping or listening to a private conversation.

Before he had listened many seconds it became quite obvious to his rapidly clearing mind that this Tuck party was a hardish case. The man who was doing the talking was saying so, very explicitly.

"From the inauspicious hour in which thou first came among us, my son, mine eye hath been dubiously upon thee, and mine ear nicely attuned unto thee. It had been better for this fair Abbey and far, far less costly, had'st thou been a swarm of locusts rather than a wandering friar. Thou hast been a vast expense to the Abbey funds and a form or species of blight to thy brethren. Nay, Friar Tuck, I exaggerate neither jot nor tittle. But yester e'en when I came upon thee and thy companions in the Refectory thou did'st shuffle the papers before thee, and right soothly and dulcetly explain that thou were instructing the others in the art of inscribing illuminated letters. It is true, Tuck, that there were illuminated letterings on pieces of vellum upon the table before thee, but thou did'st not notice, in thy unseemly haste, that thou had'st dropped upon the floor three jacks and a pair of nines! Callest thou these things examples of illuminated vellum, Friar Tuck? I am not blind, my son, and if that which was showing plainly within the hollow of thy sleeve was not yet another jack then am I no longer fit to be Abbot of this place! Upon thy habit of gluttony I do not desire to speak at great length, yet it were well to advise thee that a pack of wolves were kindlier company, because less expensive. Thou dost not fittingly regard fast days, Tuck. I do not accuse thee at random, my son, yet it is known unto me that on last fast day a leg of cold boiled pork and a fat roast capon vanished from the buttery, and no man witnessed their going. But thou wert observed in the vicinity, my son! By my soul, the man hath gone to sleep—sleeping,—*sleeping* even as I admonish him for his soul's sake! Wake up, man!"

Mr. Honey opened his eyes—to discover, what he had already begun to suspect—that *he* was the Tuck person—Friar Tuck, of the great Abbey of Soke-All by Nottingham.

"Pardon, my Lord Abbot, I but closed mine eyes the better to concentrate my faculties upon thine admonishment!" he said smoothly, for he was a ready liar. It would have sounded very convincing if unfortunately he had not punctuated the observation with a truly startling and quite unexpected hiccup.

The Abbot ignored it—in a way.

"And furthermore, Tuck, I have as ill reports of thee from the Abbey Brewster as from the establishment Distiller—and the Cellarer is frankly aghast at thee! They say that thou dost pester them beyond all reason. 'No beer, whether it be the small beer of the hinds and labourers or the noble ale for thine own table, my Lord Abbot, is safe from him,' saith the Brewster. 'From neither new beer, nor old beer, nor *any* beer, will he refrain!' And the complaint of the Distiller is this, Tuck—'He is like unto those vast and fabulous creatures that are said to eat no meat but to live by suction alone—such as dragons which are full filled of fire and seek ever to quench the same in vain. Such an one is Friar Tuck.' As for the Cellarer, he lamenteth daily thine inroads upon his wine. 'There is no wine—sweet or dry—sharp or fruity—which can be preserved from his ravening maw!'"

"Nay, pardon, my Lord Abbot, but indeed they unwittingly exaggerate. It is true, and I confess it freely unto thee, that indeed I take a little of this or that—whatsoe'er be handy—for my stomach's sake, for that I claim, humbly, my Lord, most humbly, to be but prudent and necessary for the maintenance of my health, but beyond that, my Lord Abbot, I dare not—in my state of health—venture. And concerning that leg of cold pork . . ."

Rather to Tuck's surprise the Abbot smiled—a thing the Friar had never known him do before, for he was not a smiling kind of man. It was just a little disconcerting to see a smile on that great, heavy-jowled, over-fatted face with avaricious eyes set like stones in its folds.

"Nay, my son, no more of the pork. Listen shrewdly unto me! I was minded to cast thee forth from the Abbey furnished with naught but scrip and cloak and staff to beg thy bread upon the highways. But because it is reported unto me that, despite thy manifold failings, thou art gifted with a ready wit, great powers of persuasion, and a knack of making good friends wheresoever thou goest, I am minded to forgive thee thy numberless infringements of the Abbey laws and to give thee an opportunity to re-establish thyself in my good graces. Listen unto me with all thine attention."

Greatly relieved—for the Abbot had, or said he had, power of life and death—Friar Tuck licked his dry lips unconsciously. The Abbot noticed it.

"Nay, lick not thy chops awhile—I will give thee an order to the Cellarer when I dismiss thee. Meantime, hearken!

"Within the gloomy depths of Sherwood Forest dwells an outlaw and his band—one Robin Hood, a bold and skilful scoundrel. Hast heard of him?"

"Yes, my Lord Abbot."

"Into his clutches hath fallen the Lady Marian, only daughter of mine old friend the Earl Simon de Soke, formerly the richest man of this fair realm, dead these two years gone. She is Ward of this Abbey until the day she reacheth the age of twenty-one years—and her vast possessions are in my guardianship until the same day.

Thereafter, she passeth out from my guardianship, and her possessions pass with her. Tuck, this must not be. It would be such a blow to the treasury of this Abbey that it and, with it, all of us here would be all-but if not utterly foundered. No more legs of pork for a light-fingered Friar, look you, Tuck—nor wines nor spirits nor even small beer! But water from the spring and porridge alone for the Friars, Tuck, mark ye! And naught else—naught—though they lick their lips from now until Doomsday. These then are my commands, and thou shalt obey them. Go to Sherwood Forest, find this Robin Hood's lair and use all thine art to rescue the Maid Marian from that place. Money shall be furnished thee in plenty—power to promise Hood such ransom as he demandeth within reason. That is to say, make him an offer. If, in spite of all thou canst do by fair means, he remaineth obdurate, then contrive to capture the maid and bring her here unto the Abbey. She is fair beyond words—she hath a voice like music, a face that falls not short of perfect beauty, and a figure—a figure that—well, let us not dwell upon figures in our circumstances, Tuck. I am advised of these things—I do not notice them for mine own self. Succeed and I will enrich thee—fail and, for thy sins, I will hang thee to the giant oak at the back of the buttery, yea, even if I have to send to the mariners at Harwich for a tow rope tough enough to sustain thy vast weight! Come now, what sayest thou?"

Strictly, there was not much to say about such an ultimatum. What there was to say Friar Tuck promptly said.

"My Lord Abbot, I will adventure it. It is said that I have a way with a wench . . ."

"A way with a wench! What words are these? Get thee gone and prepare thy plans, Tuck. Keep thy counsel—not a word to any living soul. And—here, thou winebibber, is the order to the Cellarer I spoke of. Be moderate—this is no case for the befuddled! Report to me when thou art ready to start. And let it be soon!"

. . . . .

Since there has never existed in any incarnation whatsoever an intelligent man who dawdled about unnecessarily in the neighbourhood of a powerful Abbot apparently quite willing to hang him on the old oak tree at the back of the buttery, Friar Tuck was well on his way before next day's sunrise. He had interviewed the Abbey Treasurer, and passed that officer through the squeezer in a fashion that made him appeal to the Abbot. Greatly to the Treasurer's surprise, his appeal was rejected, and the Friar tucked away, in secret places under his cloak, a larger sum of money than had gone out of the Abbey for many a mazy moon—save only when the King sent down for his dividends.

The Friar then borrowed a horse and cart and, armed with the Abbot's written order, interviewed the Brewster, the Distiller, the Cellarer and the Boss of the Buttery. Also the Armourer, for the holy Friar understood arms. He had not always been a Friar, though he had been almost everything else.

When, at last, he left, he could have withstood a serious siege. Quite a little company of monks had collected to see him off on what they understood to be a highly important private mission for the Lord Abbot. He was in a goodly humour, and was feeling extremely generous—for he had had a couple with each of the controllers of the hard drink departments.

"Fare ye well," he said. "It may be that many days must pass ere I return again unto ye. Therefore I remit all sums owing unto me, fairly won in fair contest. But, ere I depart, mark well these words—Draw not for a straight unless thou art open both ends! That is priceless advice! Heed it!"

And with these cryptic words the Friar quit the establishment—he hoped for ever. He travelled at a tolerably sharp gait for a man of his immense size—Abbots have been known to change their mind about parting with their money—but he lingered for a second at the top of a hill for a last look at the huge pile of Soke-All and to fling it a farewell greeting.

"Cold leg of pork, eh? Bah! Starvecrow! Farewell—a Friar's farewell unto it all!" he shouted, and turned on his heel with an adjuration to the horse to stop leaning against the cart and to put its heart into its work.

They headed for Sherwood Forest, Tuck enlivening the horse with the strains of a perfectly frightful song he had not sung since he had been a quartermaster in the army.

Three days later he passed into the gloomy shades of Sherwood—heavily armed and incompletely sober. A couple of wolves lurking in a thicket close by watched him enter the Forest and pass out of sight. Then they looked thoughtfully at each other, got up and quit the Forest. They were a pretty unscrupulous pair—but they knew when they met somebody out of their class.

It took Robin Hood's men no more than a day or so to pick the Friar up, and, since he spoke them fair and was generous with the contents of his cart, he found himself in the great outlaw's camp right speedily.

He took to Mr. Hood at first glance—for Robin, though obviously tough, was easy mannered and accustomed to treat most people as friends until he discovered them to be foes.

"Ho! It is a Friar, I perceive," said Robin. "Welcome, good Friar! What dost thou here?"

"I bear a letter from the Lord Abbot of Soke-All to the Lord of the Greenwood, Robin Hood, if thou art he!"

"Aye, marry, that am I," said Robin.

Friar Tuck produced a weighty wad of vellum which he passed over. Robin Hood spread it open and glanced at it.

"By the merry mistletoe bough, your Abbot, good Friar, seemeth not to be sparing of his words nor niggard of his ink! Let us bear this screed to one better able to read it than I!"[1]

The Friar followed him to a comfortable summer hut skilfully contrived of boughs and wattles, at the entrance to which sat one of the most magnificent blondes Tuck had ever seen in the course of a life of which eighty per cent had been devoted to blondes of various qualities—punctuated, when possible, by brunettes. She was knitting a little garment, and there was nothing about her enthusiastic greeting to Mr. Hood which suggested that she was anything but an extremely willing captive of an extremely good-looking outlaw.

Friar Tuck gravely bestowed his valuable blessing upon Maid Marian—for he was, in his way, a master of his particular technique. But he did not bless Mr. Hood—on the contrary, he offered him a drink and, his offer being enthusiastically accepted, the Friar suggested that his cart and its contents be hauled close up to the hut where it would be under the personal eye and supervision of the Captain of the merry men.

Robin agreed, and shouted an order which, while the beautiful Maid Marian pored over the Abbot's letter, was promptly obeyed. Presently, having rewarded the stalwart but thirsty-looking company of outlaws with one of the barrels, Robin Hood turned to his lovely captive and his less lovely visitor.

[1] Robin Hood could not read or write. Very few people could. Nobody had anything to read in those days, anyway. Many centuries were to elapse before authors were allowed. The only writing was done by monks. It was good, but somewhat on the pious side.—Bertram.

"Well, Dear Heart, hast succeeded in deciphering these spider-trails and fly-blows from the Abbot's quill?"

The Maid laughed, her cheeks just a trifle flushed.

"Aye, Robin, have I so," she said very clearly.

"What sayeth he?"

"He writeth like the crafty villain that he is known far and wide to be. He assumeth that I am held prisoner for ransom, and that thou art desirous not of me but of my possessions. And he maketh thee a fair offer, my Robin. As agent for the King he proffereth thee a thousand pence, a free pardon and a large farm for thyself if thou wilt but send him myself in person. A thousand pence!"[1]

She laughed contemptuously.

"Am I not worth more than a thousand pence, Robin?"

He enfolded her considerably.

"Darling, there is not, there never hath been, nor ever will be, enough gold—not to mention coppers—in this world to buy thy dear self away from me!" he told her.

Rather unprofessionally—for a holy Friar—the man Tuck broke into enthusiastic applause.

"Nobly spoken—oh, most finely said!" he cried. "The Lady Marian is answered—and, forsooth, so, too, is yon skinflint and leech, my master aforetime, the Lord Abbot of Soke-All!"

Robin Hood looked at him sharply.

"Aforetime, Friar?" he asked.

"Aye, marry," said Tuck. "It is my hope to enlist under thee, and in company with yonder gallant company of Foresters, to serve thee and thy fair Lady faithfully and well. An it be agreeable unto thee I volunteer and,

[1] It is only fair to state that a penny of those days—twelfth century—was more valuable than a penny of these days. It was worth at least twopence. But it wasn't much of a ransom for a blonde of Marian's class.—Bertram.

wit ye well, I strongly recommend myself, as private chaplain unto thee, unto thy Lady and all this goodly company of free men of the greenwood!"

Maid Marian, still in the bend of Mr. Hood's strong, protective arm, whispered something, and the outlaw nodded.

"So be it, Friar Tuck! Thou can'st consider thyself enrolled, and on the establishment. And I have awaiting thee an important task. Owing, after a fashion, to circumstances over which the Lady Marian and I have had but little control, the—um—general position here is not quite regular. Thou can'st correct this. Wilt marry us forthwith, Friar?"

"Aye, marry, that will I!" said Tuck, ignoring the fact that he had about as many legal qualifications for marrying them as he had of issuing gold coins with his own image stamped on them.

But the ceremony was postponed, for just as Hood put his horn—his blowing, not his drinking horn—to his lips to summon his band, two outlaws came up, hustling along between them a reluctant third person. He held back considerably, this one, so that they scuffled him up to Mr. Hood rather roughly. He snarled at them like a dog that they were hurting his elbows.

At the sound of his voice Friar Tuck looked closely at him. Under the mud encrusting his countenance the Friar recognised him.

He, too, was from Soke-All Abbey.

Robin Hood, who seemed to notice most things, looked at Tuck.

"Thou knowest this one, Friar?"

"Aye! It is a scurvy knave, one Tom Tosspot, an under clerk in the office of the Abbey Treasurer!" said Friar Tuck and glowered formidably upon the wilting captive. "By your leave, good Master Hood, I will e'en question the varlet!"

Robin nodded and the vast Friar turned again to the trembling Tosspot.

"Deny it not, knave, thou art a spy set upon me by the Lord Starvecrow of Soke-All—thou hast dogged my steps and the ruts of my cartwheels from Soke-All to Sherwood!"

"Nay, I have dogged thee not—I would not dog a dog, much less one so popular, so genial and well-beloved as thou art, Friar Tuck!" declared Mr. Tosspot—a meagrely modelled man, who looked half-starved. "I am a clerkly man, as thou hast said. No dogger am I, I swear it."

"Then how comest thou here? And why?" asked Robin Hood.

"I came not of mine own accord, sir—these tall archers lugged me hither with many clouts and buffets. Yet I have done no harm, desiring only to speak with thee for a little space and thereafter to journey on unto York, at which place dwelleth friends of mine who will give me shelter from the fury of the Lord Abbot if and when the Treasurer discovereth the whole of that which I have done at the Abbey!"

"And what hast thou done?" demanded Robin Hood sternly.

"Sir, it is a tale to set thee wondering that such villains can flourish!" said Mr. Tosspot nervously, sinking his voice.

"Narrate it," ordered the outlaw.

The clerk narrated fast and glibly for a full quarter of an hour without drawing breath.

It appeared that the Abbey Treasurer, for some time past, had been given to the practice of wine-bibbing—not the ordinary, every-day bibbing practised in those violent days by every man who could get hold of anything to bib, but a truly superhuman bibbing.

The wine was potent, and it had made the usual inroads upon the virtues of the Treasurer. He had become increasingly careless of his books, and had left far too much of his work to, and reposed a great deal too much trust in, his half-starved clerk. Noticing one or two discrepancies, Tosspot had gone through the books like a ferret through a rabbit warren, and tracking one discrepancy after another, had finally discovered, after months of secret, patient work, that the books, so far from merely containing a discrepancy here and there, were, for all practical purposes, one huge discrepancy in themselves.

"I swear, good sir, that, inasmuch and in so far as the truth is concerned, the books of the Abbey contain no more thereof than the whimsical and romantic songs of the troubadours and the *jongleurs*—not to mention the Welsh harpists! Prithee believe me, good Master Hood! I stated no more than the truth when I said that I am not capable to dog a man, for I am no bloodhound, but, sir, by the bread—that is to say, the Abbey crusts—by which I live I yield to no man in my ability to dog a discrepancy, for I am a clerk and such is my nature."

"And, in terms of money, Tosspot, what is the extent—the amount—of these grave and treasonable defalcations, forgeries, false entries and embezzlements?" asked Friar Tuck, deeply interested.

"Within nine years, the Lord Abbot, abetted by the Treasurer, hath, by my estimating, defrauded the King's Grace alone of as much as forty-four thousand marks! Nor doth the King suffer alone—many another hath unwittingly contributed to the plunder!"

Robin Hood looked at Friar Tuck.

"Holdest thou that this is possible, Tuck? For if the knave speaketh truly then, forsooth, it meseemeth that I and my merry men all are but bunglers and amateurs, and the starveling plunder for which we daily risk our necks is no more than fowl food—nay, less even than a grain of mustard seed . . ."

"Chicken feed thou sayest, Master Hood—and rightly so!"

"Oh, but this is a most shameful thing!" cried the indignant Maid Marian. "That thou, Robin, thou (and all these our gallant foresters) shouldest labour so hard, endure so nobly life in the Forest for sake of—how said the Friar?—chicken feed, while yon fat Abbot waxes wealthy by no more than a few crooked strokes of his drunken Treasurer's pen!"

"Can'st prove thy words, Tosspot?" asked Friar Tuck.

"Aye, that can I," said the human ferret triumphantly, and tapped his shabby doublet, from which he produced an enormous wad of parchments.

"Here is proof and proof again and proof to spare!" he said, selected one imposing document, and bowing humbly proffered it to Maid Marian.

"It is the true Will and Testament of the noble Lord Simon, thy father, mistress," he said.

Marian needed no more than one glance at it. With an exclamation of joy she showed it to Robin Hood.

"Little I dreamed ever to set eyes upon this, Robin! Knowest thou what this meaneth to us—to we two? Nay, I shall tell thee. This is the true last Will of my father. Look! Nay, no matter—I will tell thee. In this Will my father made me ward of the King, with whom he fought side by side in the Crusades. And of his possessions he bequeathed one half to me and one half to the King. Now this Will cancelled one which he made many years before appointing the Lord Abbot of Soke-All as guardian to me and to all that which my father bequeathed unto me until I came of age and full womanhood. It is clear that at the passing of my father the Abbot caused to be stolen this Will which I hold and in its place to be substituted that old Will of which I have spoken. So that the woman thou art marrying, my Robin, is Ward of Cœur de Lion and as well assured of one half of all the possessions of the Lord Simon de Soke, my father, as the King's Grace is assured of his half!"

"It is a true word, and a sooth thing!" said Friar Tuck, comfortably.

"That was the reason why I came in search of thee, good Master Hood," said the ferret, Tosspot, blandly.

"Now let it . . ." began Robin Hood, but broke off sharply as far away sounded the note of a horn.

Mr. Hood dropped Marian's hand and grabbed his long-bow.

The foresters came running in to their chief, fast, silent, self-reliant.

The horn sounded nearer—nearer yet—then the forester who had been on watch came racing into the camp.

"Robin! There cometh along the highway not a mile distant a goodly cavalcade! None more worthy of thy attention hath passed these many months. A serf whom I hailed shouted that it was the cavalcade of the King's taxgatherer making for Soke-All Abbey there to collect the King's dues!"

All the men in Lincoln green stared expectantly at their leader like hounds waiting the word to go—they feared neither King's men nor any other men—and here was a rich plunder awaiting them.

But Friar Tuck moved swiftly to Robin, speaking low and urgently.

The outlaw nodded agreement and turned to his men.

"Nay!" he said crisply. "The time hath come when we must abandon the pitiful tricks and ambushes and strategies of bunglers, amateurs and tyros! For, as good

Friar Tuck, my chaplain, saith, it may well prove that this cavalcade is that not of the lesser but of the greater taxgatherer, the King's Grace himself! If it so be, then, my hawks, we fly this day at greater game than ye have ever dreamed on!"

"True, true, my son," said Tuck urgently. "It is known that the Lion-Heart seeketh desperately in all directions for money wherewith to launch him upon a new Crusade against the accursed infidel. What more likely than that he should come direct for his royal dues, and as much more as he can get, from this rich Abbey! How willing an ear will he lend unto thy tale, and my tale, and especially the tale of the Lady Marian!"[1]

He turned almost savagely on Tom Tosspot.

"But thou, Tosspot, hold thy peace when thou art in the King's presence—speak not until thou art bidden to speak—or, mark it well, thy end will be swift and dismal."

Robin addressed a few words to his band and, hand in hand with Maid Marian, followed closely by his chaplain, led the way to the high road along which the cavalcade was travelling.

. . . . .

From behind the leafy screen of the trees and thickets the merry men of Sherwood studied the approaching cavalcade, but keen-eyed though they were, they had among them one who was keener-eyed still—keener-eyed, by dint of much practice, than any man has a right to be—namely, the hard-bitten sharp-set Tuck.

"By my faith, Robin," he muttered in a few moments, "this cavalcade is too splendid and glittering for a lousy

[1] Tuck was about right. From the day he came to the throne to the day he vacated it Richard the First was hard-up. He never got as much as he needed, though he did his best, and was not too choosey about his methods.—Bertram.

taxgatherer! An' the Lion-Heart rideth not among them then mine eyes are not what they were aforetime."

He took another long stare.

"Aye—there he rideth. It is the King's Grace himself!" He sighed with relief, and mopped his brow.

"This, an' I miss not my guess, is thy lucky day, Robin. Now I counsel thee, leave all to me, and keep thy lads in check unseen until I call upon thee and thy Lady Marian."

Then, when the cavalcade was all-but abreast of them, the Friar stepped quietly into the road.

His sudden appearance caused no stir nor aroused any suspicion. Wandering Friars were as common as pigs' tracks on a pig farm in those days. Nobody interfered with them—in fact, people appeared rather to like seeing them around. They often made themselves useful to the sick, they could tell or invent a good story, frequently they could sing a good song, and they were usually welcome to share the evening meal with anyone who had an evening meal to share or a bed with anyone who had a bed to share.

Even as the lynx-eyed Tuck had seen, King Richard the First rode at the head of the cavalcade. It was a tough, hard-boiled cavalcade, and it had a tough, hard-boiled leader. Cœur de Lion was tall and broad and big enough to cause his great black charger to grunt a little when he flung himself about in his saddle, as he frequently did. He was as handsome as a handsome bull elephant when he smiled—less handsome when he frowned. He was wearing about forty-five pounds of burnished chain mail and he carried a light battleaxe of about twenty pound weight, not because he was needing an axe just then, but because he was as accustomed to carry an axe around as a Cabinet Minister is accustomed to carry an umbrella, and felt a little naked without it.

A grim Royalty, Richard.

But Friar Tuck was accustomed to grimness, as most men who have knocked about the world became, and it was without hesitation that he halted in the middle of the road and gravely bestowed his valuable blessing on the King and all his enterprises. Richard listened with well-feigned interest.

"Our thanks, good Friar," he said. "Give him a groat!" he added to his treasurer, and would have ridden on, but Tuck spoke rapidly:

"May it please your Majesty to deign to lend thy royal ear to tidings of great import . . ."

"Nay, nay—time presses. Stand aside!" shouted the impatient king.

But Tuck continued imperturbably—

"—concerning very large sums of money which have been wrongfully withholden from the Royal Treasury by evildoers whom I and my associates have but recently tracked down!"

"Eh? What sayest thou, Friar! *Money*—large sums of money withholden from our Treasury!"

His piercing eyes transfixed the Friar.

"I am well assured that I speak truly, my Lord King! To quote but one item of forty-four thousand marks alone . . ."

The King foamed a little.

"Tellest thou us that there liveth in this fair realm a knave so dastard, so bold, that he dareth to withhold so vast a sum from our Privy Purse!" he bawled. "By the splendour of God, thou shalt prove thy charges, Friar, or shalt be flayed alive! What! Am I not King of this land, yea, and foremost Crusader of all! Know ye not that such money would go far to equip me an army? Hast witnesses to this terrible crime?"

"Aye, my Lord King, that have I," returned the Friar.

"Name him!"

"He is known as Robin Hood, my Lord King."

"An outlaw! Thou chucklehead! What is the value of an outlaw's word?"

Tuck laughed.

"As I estimate it, at a rough guess, peradventure that value well may prove to be another thirty thousand marks—being none other than one half of his lady wife's estate!"

"Another thirty thousand marks! God's wounds, we have arrived in a fair place at a fitting hour!" swore Richard. "Who, then, is this lady wife of the outlaw—and where doth she abide?"

"As to the first question, my Lord King, she is the Lady Marian, only daughter of the dead Earl Simon de Soke . . ."

Again the bruiser King swore one of his tremendous oaths.

"Simon! Simon de Soke! Mine old comrade on many a bloody field! I knew not he had either son or daughter!"

"A daughter only—wife of Robin Hood," said Friar Tuck, smoothly. "In the Earl Simon's last Will and Testament he bequeathed unto thee, my Lord King, one half of his whole vast estate . . ."

"Aye, Simon was ever one for the loot, and that which he had he held ever," muttered Richard, smiling at some memory or another.

"And his lovely lady daughter to be the King's ward—at the King's pleasure!"

"And, 'fore God, my pleasure it is, Friar! Ah, my gallant old Simon—*there* was an Earl who remembered what was due to his King!"

His steely glare swept across the faces of the Earls and Barons all about him.

"Would to God I had more such Earls as he! The half of his estate, sayest thou! That is music to mine ear—would the Saracen could hear it!"

Then the wily Friar called Robin and the Lady Marian.

Cœur de Lion looked curiously at Hood.

"So! Thou art the outlaw of whom the tales are told. Thou art a seemly man—would'st be better employed shooting the infidel than my Sherwood deer, man."

"Outlaw so-called, my Lord King—but by rumour alone, for never have I been legally outlawed. And I am a King's man, like my father-in-law before me, and sworn enemy to all whom I know guilty of dipping a secret hand into the King's Treasury!"

"Well said!"

The eagle eyes pounced on Marian and softened.

"Greeting, my child—thou wild, beautiful thing!" said Richard with a great laugh. "So thou art my ward and my co-heir to mine old comrade Simon's estates! Aye, I see it—thou hast his blue eyes and a certain straight look! I loved thy father, child! And I love thee—and thine husband, outlaw or none, I heartily approve. Scrivener!"

A scrivening kind of man came forward.

"In-law me this man forthwith!"

The scrivener began to scribe like a man in a hurry.

The King turned to Robin Hood and the Friar.

"Ye know where lieth the money that was first spoken of?" he demanded.

They bowed.

"It is in the possession of the traitor Abbot of Soke-All—he who hath embezzled the same over many years, my Lord King!" said Tuck.

The King commanded a palfrey to be brought for Marian, and invited her to ride at his side.

"We will e'en interview the Abbot of Soke-All," said Richard softly, then thought of something.

"Thy band of merry men, Robin Hood! Hast forgotten them?"

"Nay, my Lord King! It is in my mind that, by thy good leave, I will e'en throw them forward as a screen to surround the Abbey and prevent the escape of the Abbot with his plunder!"

"Art a soldier, I perceive! A goodly thought."

Robin blew his horn, and the men in Lincoln green poured from the thickets.

Richard, for a fleeting second, seemed startled at their numbers and quality.

"By the Splendour of the Heavens, Robin Hood, now I know thee for a true King's man—for hadst thou been otherwise thou would'st have had us in an ambush against which it would have gone hard to prevail. Those bows are no toys for children, and there is a vicious gleam to their arrowheads that would well reflect the glare of the sun of the Holy Land!" he hinted. "Advance your screen!"

Robin gave the necessary orders, and the company of green-clad bowmen vanished silently into the thickets from whence they had appeared, running silent like wolves.

"Robin, I could use thy company on my next Crusade," he said, hintfully.

Friar Tuck spoke.

"My Lord King, grant me to speak for Robin, who is a modest man. I am assured that if it should be thy wish to take the Abbey of Soke-All for thyself, and to set in command of it Robin Hood to make of it a garrison or as it may be a species of barracks, there would he train ye well-nigh as many men as thine heart could desire!"

"Would'st do that, Robin?" asked Richard.

"Aye, marry, my Lord King, right joyously!" said Robin Hood.

"So be it! And I, for my part, shall make of thee an Earl—not Earl of Nottingham, for there is already one of these, but Earl of Huntingdon shalt thou be, and thy men shall be forever after known as the Sherwood Foresters![1] And now—Forward! Report to me at the Abbey, Robin, and fear not but that I will care for thy sweet bride till then!"

The cavalcade moved on.

Robin followed his men.

Friar Tuck stood by the side of the road, mopping his brow.

He was charmed at the results he had so swiftly engineered, but he was too thirsty to think. He waited till the King's Vintner came along with his wagon of wine casks. This vehicle he stopped. Rumours of his discourse with the King had already reached the Vintner, and the casks were freely at his disposal.

"Wine, good Vintner, wine. Floods of it—Sherris to begin with. With what I will finish I will advise thee later!"

He heard the clink of a huge silver goblet and reached for it—only to discover that he, Hobart Honey—had moved his arm suddenly as the power of the pill waned, and he woke to find he had broken the port glass against the decanter.

He took another glass from the cupboard and sat for a while wondering rather wistfully what had happened to him after he had refreshed himself at the Vintner's wine-wagon.

He had no doubt that all had gone well—but it was a pity that the power of the pill had waned so soon.

Then it occurred to him that even as he sat in his

[1] Later—a few centuries later—they became known in the British Army as the 45th and 95th Foot (Robin Hood Rifles). Nowadays they are known by their original title, viz.: The Sherwood Foresters.—Bertram.

comfortable flat the Sherwood Foresters were probably fighting somewhere or other in the world-war for freedom—even as, after their fashion, they had fought in the twelfth century.

He raised his glass and drank deep to them, wherever they were.

COMMENTARY

ON

THE ADVENTURE CALLED ABBOT'S ENVOY

Hobart Honey quite obviously was greatly gratified by my portrait of him when he was Friar Tuck. He lost himself completely in his perusal of the written account of the adventure he had so recently helped in real life to enact.

"Typical Atkey *picaresque* stuff!" I heard him mutter after a few pages. "Yet somehow . . . Humph! Yes—he's got the Abbot exactly. Meanest man that ever entered a refectory. Hounded into theft by his appalling avarice. You could see it in his cold eye and icy smile. I shall never regret I was instrumental in securing his ejection from the Abbey. Marian. Ah, Marian, if only Robin had not seen you first verily I believe I would have abandoned the Friar's frock and re-enlisted in the Army—on the chance of winning you. But that's a dream, child. You were not for the likes of old Friar Tuck. No, no—I was a born bachelor—adventurer—wanderer—vagrant. It was better so—could not by any conceivable chance have been otherwise. You and Robin were born for each other. Lord, how I loved the man—so bold, so quick, so light—so competent and yet so kindly. Even Richard loved him within a few moments of their meeting. And I, myself,—not too bad, I venture to claim—a little unscrupulous maybe—yes, a little—but capable under my

Friar's frock. I shall not forget that little qualm up the small of my back when I halted the Lion-Heart's cavalcade that day. A fierce and hasty man. 'Give him a groat!' he said. And so easily it might have been, 'Clout me him into the ditch!' Yes, it called for more courage than one would easily believe—we Friars were ten a penny in those days! I wonder why—after all, it was a hard life—harder than that of chaplain to Robin, Earl of Huntingdon, hoho! and Colonel of the gallant old Sherwood Foresters! Yes, a success—a fortunate pill—morals apart."

Hobart ceased his mutterings and dragged himself reluctantly from his shady past.

"Excellent, my dear Bertram—you have helped me to restore my own faith in my integrity!"

"I am glad of that," I said, "though I don't quite see your point. Surely, I have depicted Tuck as a tolerably tough old crook, devoid of any sort of integrity—about as honourable as a starving timber wolf and with morals as steadfast as those of a scalded tom-cat."

Rather to my surprise Honey only smiled.

"In the reign of Richard the First there were many traits or habits to which we did not attach the importance which is attached to them nowadays," he said blandly. "No, frankly, I am delighted, Bertram. Help yourself to a drink and pass the decanter."

I had already done so. *I* may never have been Friar Tuck, personally, nor even a pupil of that adroit old ruffian—but at least I was sufficiently intelligent to assist myself to a little gentlemanly stimulant without waiting for Honey to finish his paean to the already fading phantom of Robin Hood's self-styled "chaplain."

BERTRAM.

THE FOURTEENTH PILL

DEATH TO THE HUN

THERE followed for Hobart Honey a sequence of three pills which produced nothing whatever in the least worthy of putting on record in any detailed form.

He spent the whole of one of these incarnations as a denizen of one of the Great Deeps known to exist in the Pacific Ocean—none other than a superb specimen of the Great Spotted Thousand-jointed Jigsaw Lobster, a melancholy and complicated monster which, throughout the whole duration of the power of the pill, sat in a small cave about the size of a large hole, taking itself to pieces and putting itself together again, never twice in the same way and never rightly. Another of these pills afforded him a brief experience of life as a young *cobra di capello* in India—from the miseries of which he was abruptly removed by a large and hungry secretary bird—a stork-like creature remarkable chiefly for the good use it makes of a depraved appetite.

And the third pill gave him an intimate knowledge of life as a rare flowering cactus in the Sonora desert. All he remembered of this incarnation was the fact that he possessed a far more exquisite perfume then than he possessed in his present incarnation.

Then came a pill the results of which he considered well worthy of recording.

It was perhaps a fortnight after his experience in Sherwood Forest when, one evening, he felt particularly anxious for a temporary change from this life. He had had a hard and rather dull day's work, and as soon as he had dined he settled himself comfortably in his chair, wished away a glass of port, swallowed a pill at random, and washed it onwards with a second port—quite as usual.

"Anything for a change!" he murmured as his Adam's apple performed. "To put it no higher than that!"

He laughed drowsily.

Then all was black and silent. At least, for a moment he believed it to be so, but he was wrong, for, almost immediately he heard a voice—the lovely, dreamlike, luscious voice of a woman. For a second it sounded as if she were far-off, then he knew that she was close at hand. . . .

"I have sent expressly for thee to comfort me, and to assuage mine heart's desire!"

He opened his eyes instantly—to gaze upon the lady who had sent for him. It would have been quite understandable if he had closed them again as instantly, for she was undeniably dazzling. She was reclining in a lightly-clad sort of fashion upon a silken couch under a window that admitted the rays of a setting sun, and she was beautiful, with a darkling and tropical beauty that was superlative even in the Rome of A.D. 461.

She was extremely voluptuous—excusably so, for, though it was no longer quite what it had been, Rome was still a reasonably voluptuous place.

She was staring at him with the skilled appraisement of a highly-experienced woman.

"Yes," she said. "Thou art a man of singularly seemly appearance, Obarton. . . . Draw close the curtains! Turn the key in the lock of the door! Speak low. I wish to talk to thee of Love and serious things!"

Mr. Honey, or, as he was now, in this incarnation, Obarton the Arranger, drew close the curtain, turned the key in the lock of the door and, when it was his turn to speak, spoke low.

But he had no illusions about the lady. He had never

seen her before. Though he had heard of her—and what he could see of her now bore out everything he had ever heard of her.

She was Augusta Honoria, princess daughter of the Empress Placidia, the sister of Valentinian, the Roman Emperor.

It was now universally accepted as a Truth of the first grade that Honoria literally lived for love. It was the way she was.[1]

Obarton was completely familiar with her life and times, so to express it, and he did not, of course, for a single second commit the *faux pas* of imagining that Love in her mind was bracketed with him. On the contrary, she had sent for him on a matter of business—very strict business indeed. He was a well-known Arranger, with his head office in Rome and a branch in Constantinople.

For a few moments she lay thinking, her eyes absently on Obarton. For his part he stood waiting, his eyes less absently on her. She was wondering exactly how to start the interview—Obarton was figuring about how much her income was.

He ran her history over in his mind as he waited, and he was conscious at once of a good deal of sympathy for her. She had been well under sixteen when they bestowed the title of *Augusta* on her—which title put her completely out of the class of any husband but a Royal one. Apparently the girl's experience of the current Royalties had not been so delightful that she wished for one for her own, and, a year or two later, she had fallen in a truly Roman way for one Eugenius, a regular fellow, who happened to be her chamberlain. All went well for a time. Then, as is customary in these affairs, all went less well. Honoria's

[1] The late Mr. Edward Gibbon, author of the engaging little tome entitled *The Decline and Fall of the Roman Empire*, entirely agrees with me about this.—Bertram.

mother, the formidable Placidia, intervened. These were the days when intervention *was* intervention, and the ardent Honoria was exiled to Constantinople, where she spent the next ten or twelve years in what she regarded as somewhat dreary seclusion among the Virgins connected with the court of Theodosius—a seclusion that had been so strictly enforced that the historians suggest that Honoria went wellnigh *crackerissimo*. She certainly became desperate. She had gathered a good many odd scraps of information about the conquering Hun of that period, one Attila—certainly a rising man, and said by practically everybody who was afraid of him—and most people were—to have a colossal future. His reputation in Rome and Constantinople was rising like a kite. Either ignoring, or, more likely not knowing, the real class of this barbarian rough, the desperate princess sent her favourite eunuch in secret to the mighty Hun, offering herself in marriage. She knew nothing about him—she could not even speak his language—but anything that could get her away from her seclusion and all it implied went with Honoria—not without a certain amount of reason, for ten solid years of fasting and vigils in what the historians call "the irksome society of the sisters of Theodosius and their chosen virgins" can easily be imagined to be something of a trial to a high-spirited princess of about twenty-six.

And Attila declined her without thanks.

It hurt.

She, *Augusta* Honoria, sister of the Emperor, passed up by a Hun barbarian and multi-murderer! She may have been feeling lonely but she had her pride. She never forgot it—and certainly never forgave it. Shortly after that it became obvious to her home folk at Rome that the girl had pretty well served her time, anyway. They had her back to Rome, where she gave herself a hearty welcome, and was thoroughly enjoying her life and times when suddenly who but Attila, from motives of sheer avarice and political expediency, demanded her as the latest of his innumerable wives—plus, he particularly stated, the last cent of her Imperial dowry.

With the exception of that part of the foregoing which concerned Attila the Hun, Obarton knew most of the story of Honoria's troubles.

At last, the Princess broke the silence.

"Thou knowest my sad history, Arranger?"

"Often have I wept in secret for thy sufferings, Augusta," said Obarton.

She shrugged her beautiful shoulders.

"But *all* thou canst not know. We talk now in deep secret, Obarton. Know now that once, in despair, I offered myself as wife to Attila the Hun—secretly!"

"The Scourge of God!"[1] Obarton felt a chill pass up his spine at the sound of the hated name.

"To escape my exile! He disdained me then. . . . *Now* he hath sent to Rome demanding me—and the Emperor, my brother, and my mother, the Empress Placidia, are deeply affronted at the insolence of this barbarian. They will refuse him, and there will be bitter war. He will bring his hordes to the very gates of Rome. *Obarton, they must never know that I once offered to wed Attila!*"

"He will tell them!" said Obarton.

"Nay—if he is dead how then can he tell them?"

"But he is not dead!"

"I know," cooed the Princess. "This is why I sent for thee, Obarton. Thou advertiseth thyself as an Arranger, dost thou not?"

Obarton admitted it, reluctantly.

[1] Some say that Tamerlane was the Scourge of God. The truth is that both were. Each murdered about the same number of millions of ordinary folk.—Bertram.

"As an Arranger thou understandest the peradventures of life and the distant goal of life, which is death, dost thou not? Thou hast been commended to me as one who, for a price, can arrange all things. Thou art familiar with the arts of the assassin, the crafts of the *bravo,* the dark by-ways of the killers. At a price! At a price! And thou shalt receive such a price as neither thou nor any such Arranger as thou art hath ever known if thou canst but arrange for me the end of this Hunnish werewolf before he comes to Rome to take me—and mine!"

"Gods! But it is to kill the conqueror of all Europe!"

"And all Europe will thank thee on its knees."

"Oh, Princess, this thing I must consider well! Give me time!"

"Time! Time!—there is a bitter limit to the time—as there is *no* limit to the reward. Go! Think! Be swift! Come back when thou art prepared! Unlock the door—call my treasurer! Thou can'st not think without gold. It is ready for thee—an abundance. . . . Succeed in this mission, Obarton, and I will enrich thee and"—her eyes flashed above a brilliant smile—"thou shalt be forever established in my favour!"

Obarton bowed and unlocked the door. After all, he was a man of business—rough or smooth. And this talk of cash in advance was as minstrelsy to his ear. About being established in her favour later on he was not so sure. She was very beautiful after her fashion—but so is a sleek, young tigress, after hers.

. . . . .

To this day the name of Attila stinks in the nostrils of all right-minded men—though not, perhaps, so intensely as Attila did personally in the days of Valentinian. He was one of the first of the Super-Killers, and, like most of these, he was extravagantly well-guarded.

It only took the gold-gorged Obarton a few seconds to realise that he had accepted from the Princess Honoria a commission that was worth a big fee. A little further reflection convinced him that he had undertaken to perform a very considerable miracle—one which literally millions of men before him had failed to perform. But, having accepted it, he had to do something about it, or return Honoria's money—an expedient which was not, never had been, and was extremely unlikely ever to become a part of his business method.

"Huh!" he said to himself over a goblet of old vintage Falernian that evening. "Often have I longed to be in the Big Money! Now I am in it. But, by the gods, I could find it within me to wish I were out of it!"

But a few more goblets cheered him up a little. He took a look at himself in a burnished silver mirror. Even as the promising Princess had said, he was a singularly seemly Arranger. If he had lived in these days he almost certainly would have been functioning at Hollywood. But Hollywood was so much a thing of the far future that it might just as well have been a thing of the far past.

Another goblet convinced him that, after all, there was something to be said for a vista in which he saw himself as an established favourite of the sister of the Emperor Valentinian—who was fond of her, and now that the Empress Placidia was getting older and much less influential, not to say formidable, able to do for her anything in reason that she wanted done. Money would cease to matter. The arranging business could be sold and forgotten. Yes, definitely a prospect.

He sent for one of the few men he could trust.[1] This was

[1] In those cheerful days you had to know a man about twenty years, as well as having a hold on him, before you trusted him. Then he probably double-crossed you. . . . Brutus, a patrician of ancient Rome, in his little volume of memoirs, *Looking Back At it All*, agrees with me, though he was not a man I, personally, would trust.—Bertram.

Bullo, who in his day had personally conducted a big business as a professional murderer. For years he had been the best and most highly paid *bravo* in Rome but, growing old and careless, he had so grossly mismanaged a commission to exterminate a well-known Goth that when, by sheer luck, he managed to crawl into the darkness out of reach of the annoyed Goth, he left about thirty-two and a half per cent of his working parts behind him. Bullo had then retired from active business, though he still did a little as a Consulting Murderer, and had established himself as a competent Professor of Poisons. He still had brains in his head—the Goth must have overlooked these—and, of course, enormous experience.

Obarton sent for him on the off-chance that Bullo, a notorious Hun-hater, might stew up an idea.

Bullo, fresh from his favourite tavern, was in a talkative mood when he lurched over to Obarton's place, and he was more so before he had had a couple of the unwatered Falernian wine the Arranger plentifully provided.

But, even so, he was not really enthusiastic.

"Mark ye, Obarton, it is a difficult and complicated technique. None but a genius, with a desire to perform suicide, would undertake the extinction of Attila. For myself, I—yea, even I, Bullo—have invariably refused all offers to subtract Attila from the total Hun population. His bodyguard is what any ordinary King would describe as an army—and he, himself, is as cunning as a wolf, as savage as a wild bull, and as quick to strike as a snake—quicker, indeed, for snakes, in my experience, are slow in the strike, and their timing is bad. I never used them except in cheap cases, when the out-of-pocket expenses had to be kept low. Moreover, the Hun king is a wizard with horses—he liveth his life on horseback—and it is said that all of his horses are trained to kick backward with their hind legs or punch forward with their front legs at a touch. With their teeth they are taught to snap like a rat-trap—but quicker. Nay, Obarton, leave well alone. It is less a contract for a man than a woman, for, mark ye well, it is conceivable that there may be moments when he will relax in company with a woman—but in the company of no man hath he ever been known to lay aside his caution. They say that ever his pig-eyes rove from face to face of even his favourite generals—nay, leave well alone, Obarton!"

Bullo downed a goblet.

"Or if thou art set upon it, remember these words of Bullo—yea, I, Bullo himself, who speaketh unto thee—'Never lived the man who was match for the woman of his life. For, observe it well, Obarton, one man is one life, but within his one life are many women. They loom in the orbit of his one life like a multitude of blossoms,[1] and though he may pluck them by the myriad, yet always in the end one of them shall pluck him!' There—*hic*—" Bullo passed his goblet for replenishment, "let us seek among the fair ones in Attila's life for the one who shall forever finish it. And the sooner the better."

"Thou art a philosopher—of a kind—I perceive," said Obarton sourly. Nevertheless he was attracted by Bullo's reasoning—and began to talk in terms of money—cold money down and quite a lot of it.

"I shall not offend thee, good Bullo, if I say that thy business is of a more popular grade than mine. Mine is more exclusive, and my fees are vastly in excess of thine. Therefore thou hast to do with the many whereas I do with the few. Enquire discreetly among thy cut-throat *clientele*—as the Franks say—concerning possibilities. Here is gold and, mark ye well, my Bullo, there is plenty more where that came from!"

[1] True—of that period. They were a polygamous lot. Things would have changed a good deal since then, I take it.—Bertram.

Bullo's eyes glittered glassily.

"I will do my best, Obarton—and my best is very good indeed!" . . .

A week or so later, quite a little company of men and horses under Obarton's command, with Bullo coming a good second in command, were heading for the so-called palace of Attila on the banks of the Danube.

The men of this expedition were moderate, and not more heavily armed than the average workmen of the period, but the horses were superb—Arabs, and good ones.

It was an excellent idea, for it was about the only way in which Obarton & Co. could hope to get anywhere near Attila. His legions of toughs swarmed, miles deep, around his headquarters, and every man of them was a horse-master—had lived on horseback and on the horses, too, from childhood. Their favourite roast was a haunch of horse, their favourite *entrée* was a species of omelette of horses' blood and herbs, their favourite drink was fermented mares' milk. All other food was about as attractive to them as a bale of asparagus is to a man-eating tiger, or a strawberry shortcake is to a famished vampire bat. So eclipsed of horses was the mental horizon of the blood-hungry Huns that the leading Roman scientists of the day maintained that it was a grave oversight of Nature not to have made a thorough job of it, and had them born as horses in the first place. Or, at least, as jackasses. They would have been less blood-thirsty, and probably would have enjoyed life more.

Bullo had brought him from the underworld a rumour upon which—for lack of anything better—Obarton had gambled.

And when they were but one day's journey from Attila's H.Q. this rumour was confirmed.

They pulled in at a biggish farm, which was obviously that of a horse-raiser, and were greeted by the owner of the ranch—a seriously battered but still good-looking gentleman on crutches—one Stylo, who might have been a gipsy before he settled down to work. He was young, and clad in many colours, and had a slight acquaintance with Bullo, who promptly introduced Obarton and produced wineskins.

Stylo invited them to eat with him.

Long before the meal was over, and the frequently renewed supply of wineskins was exhausted, they were talking both freely and frankly.

"Thou hast suffered an accident recently, Stylo," said Obarton, as he tilted a wineskin for his battered host.

"Aye, Obarton, that have I—at the hands of one of Attila's captains, Dagga, a man like a bear. My foot slipped at a critical moment or it would have been otherwise. *He* would have qualified for the crutches. Doubtless it was the will of the gods—and my unlucky day. But when I am healed up we shall meet again!" said Stylo, his eyes grim.

"It was a private quarrel?" asked Obarton, politely.

"If to leave a man for dead and to abduct his betrothed can be called a quarrel, it was," snarled Stylo. "That was the way of it, look you. In two days' time Ildico, the loveliest woman in the world, would have been my wife. But I was not the only one who appreciated her charms. This raider, this Hun woman-stealer, appreciated her also, and, as is their way, he came here with another like him, and took us by surprise. Me they left for dead, Ildico they bore away. Rumour hath come to me since that evil day that it was not because *he* coveted her that Dagga came—but because of a hint let fall by none other than Attila, the Hun King himself, who had seen her while riding one day."

"Attila! Gods! Then there is no hope?" exclaimed Bullo.

Stylo eyed him dourly.

"While there is life there is at least hope—of death—somebody's!" he said with a note under-running his voice which would have startled anyone less hard-boiled than Obarton and partner. "For, mark ye well, friends, Ildico is no witless bird of Paradise! Nay, she is supple and fierce and cunning—she comes of true gipsy stock—she is like a beautiful, dangerous snake of venomous steel—and it is I, Stylo, who am her heart's desire, as she is mine!" He hissed the last words at them, more than a little snakishly himself.

The Arranger and the murderer exchanged glances and rose.

"We ourselves are bound for Attila's palace, and it may befall that we have opportunity to speak with her. Who knows?" said Obarton. "Hast any message—or aught to send her, Stylo?"

"Aye, that have I!" The gipsy hobbled to a corner of the apartment and fumbled at a skin bag which lay on a stool. Returning, he gave Obarton several quills each coloured differently.

"If thou canst get these quills into her hands, with word that from this hour onwards there will, for the next six moons, be awaiting here, ready to leave in an instant, my fastest horses, then I will give thee this farm and all thereon. More I cannot give for I have no more!"

Bullo stared at the quills.

"Poisons?"

"Poisons from Egypt!" said Stylo, darkly.

"The Egyptian are usually good poisons—I know them *all*!" observed Bullo.

But he spoke otherwise when, a little later, they rode on.

"Concerning the poisons, Stylo spoke truly," he said. "These Egyptian poisons are good—swift, subtle, portable and inexpensive. Suitable for amateurs. But I do not use them for the better class of case. Most of them are easily diagnosed by a skilful physician. It is otherwise with those I use for my more expensive contracts!"

He chuckled—much as one would expect a diamond-back rattler to chuckle if, indeed, they ever do.[1]

Obarton did not chuckle. He seemed a little uncomfortable. But he answered civilly enough.

"Thou art famous as a master of thine art, Bullo," he said, his smile a little forced. "Now, for an example, let us suppose that we have the good fortune to meet with the beautiful Ildico, and are able to convey to her hands a—er—form of release for the Hun King, which of thy wide assortment would'st thou, as a high-class professor or purveyor of sudden death, proffer unto her?"

Again the skin-crawling chuckle from the "Professor."

"Without hesitation, just one small pellet of my Arabian Powder No. 2. It is so small that one can hold it invisible between the bases of any two fingers so that one may drop it unseen where and when one will. It acts like lightning, but it leaves no trace. There lives not the physician who can say, 'This person died of Bullo's Arabian Powder No. 2.' And if there were a physician who could he would not live very long!"

"Hah!" said Obarton. "And how doth this delectable powder act that it should leave no trace?"

"It bursteth the arteries of whoso taketh it," said Bullo casually, and pulled up abruptly as they were halted by a gang of Hun horsemen who challenged them.

"Whither goest thou with these horses?" demanded the leader. He had already grabbed the headropes of one of the best, and his men, horse-thieves by birth, upbringing and natural inclination, were reaching for theirs as Obarton's answer rasped out.

[1] Buffon agrees with me that chuckling rattlesnakes are very rare. They have very little to chuckle about.—Bertram.

"These be horses from the deserts of Arabia, a gift from the great Estyloh, Sheik of Deytvil, unto His Majesty King Attila. Each horse is branded in a secret place with the brand of Great Attila—and—it were better for any horse-thief that he should flay himself alive than touch or hinder the passage of these noble beasts to the stables of His Majesty!"

The clutching hands of the Huns fell away as though the halters were white-hot. Even the hard-boiled captain of the crew looked scared.

"Pass, pass! In the name of all the gods, pass on!" he growled. "We were but admiring the noble brutes! Way! Make way, thou swine, there! Way for the King's Arabians!"

Nobody else hindered them—for Attila was notoriously rough with people who interfered with his horses.

. . . . .

All went well—far better, indeed, than Obarton had expected. Attila was away deleting a town (and its inhabitants) which had offended him. He would return that afternoon in time for the quick ceremony which would add Ildico to his already extensive list of wives. Most of the swarming Huns were already half-drunk in anticipation of the festivities. They would be unconscious by the time the brief marriage ceremonies were completed.

The Arab horses were the subject of great admiration, and Obarton & Co. were welcomed. Apartments in the so-called palace were reserved for them, and they did a good deal of drinking with Manour, the ancient, bow-legged tough who called himself Master of the King's Horse. This person had fallen utterly and completely for the Arabs. The numberless Tartar ponies of the Huns were tough and enduring, but they were nothing to look at, and their action was little better than that of a motor-cycle flat on both tyres. They were hardly the same species of mammal as the Arabs. Manour had tried a few of the latter and was enraptured.

"It is not riding—it is dreaming!" he said, which was pretty fair for a Hun. They were drinking late, and Manour was getting confidential. Cunning and suspicious as he was by nature, it never occurred to him to doubt the *bona fides* of men who brought such horses as a gift to Attila.

"There is nothing that my master will not do for ye for so good a gift," he declared. "Ye have come at a good hour, moreover, for within a few hours of his return he taketh another bride! There will be great festivities!"

"A bride! Hath the Princess Honoria arrived?" asked Obarton. "I knew not that——"

"Nay, nay—not the Princess Honoria! That is a great affair—an alliance which must be the matter of negotiation between kings. It is true that these are afoot, but the marriage of which I speak is a matter of less import! It is a girl, Ildico, who hath caught the King's taste and fancy. She will do well enough until the alliance with the sister of the Roman Emperor is made."

Manour laughed, reaching for his drinking horn.

"One more or less—what matter?"

"I have heard that she is surpassingly beautiful, Ildico," said Obarton. "Would that I could see her?"

"That can be arranged—at a price," said Manour. "Inscribe on thy parchments that the chestnut mare with the white near foreleg is designed as a gift for the King's Master of Horse and I doubt not that I can persuade Ildico to come hither to speak with thee."

"That will I do, for thou art a man after mine own heart! Good Bullo, pass me the parchment of the horses!"

Bullo, who was picking his teeth lightly—very lightly indeed—with a coloured quill, made haste to oblige.

Obarton wrote, Manour peering over his shoulder at the words he could not read.

"That maketh the chestnut mare mine, subject to Attila's approval?"

"Undoubtedly!" swore Obarton.

"Good—I go. Thou shalt see the bride!"

He went out.

Bullo leaped into activity. Moving like a conjurer, he filled Manour's drinking horn, added a little something to it, and set it back. Obarton watched the Professor engaged on his business with a comradely interest.

"There is that within the draught which will clout him senseless in a space of seconds," hissed Bullo. "Drink to the bride, Obarton, as swiftly as good manners will permit!"

Obarton nodded—wiping a sudden cold sweat from his brow.

"Gods! If Attila but knew he would crucify us, having first removed and burnt our hides!"

He pulled himself together and filled his drinking horn personally—leaving Bullo to fill his own.

"Thou hast the quills, Bullo?"

"Nay, she will not need the cheap Egyptian stuff. I shall furnish her with the best—*mine own*!" hissed Bullo, and lolled back as there entered to them a magnificent brunette, tall, lithe, graceful, vivid, with great black eyes that gleamed with a lambent and perilous light—Ildico, Attila's most recent prey.

Behind her lurched the Master of Horse.

Obarton and Bullo bowed low before her.

"Thou art the men with the Arabians sent as gift to the King by the Sheik Estyloh!" she said. But she pronounced "Estyloh" as if there were little or no "E" in it—so that it sounded almost like "Stylo."

Obarton knew, then, that she was indeed swift and subtle, as Stylo, her "heart's desire," had said.

"Even so," he said. "From Estyloh!" He, too, muted the "E." Then he took his drinking horn.

"Permit that we drink to the most beautiful bride-to-be of the Great Attila—thou, Bullo—thou, Manour, and I, Obarton!"

They drank—and Manour dropped like a pole-axed ox.

Leaving him to lie they worked fast then.

"We are from Stylo—of the farm. Trust us, Ildico."

Bullo passed her some tiny pills.

"Listen! Here are pellets! Drop one of these into the cup of wine which thou wilt proffer the tyrant when he comes to thee after the carouse on his wedding night and flee. We shall await thee with horses at the back of the palace—fear not—all the guards will be drunk! Dost understand? Quick!"

She was quick—the pills vanished. Bullo held a phial under the nostrils of Manour, and the man gave a violent shudder, opening his eyes instantly. His head rolled on the white arm of the woman.

"Awake, Manour!" she said in a dove-gentle voice.

Manour awoke.

"Drink this! Thou hast been—overcome. A passing thing, Manour—it passes! Already thou art thyself again!" crooned Bullo.

It was so.

Manour drained the cup Bullo proffered—and was himself (such as he was) again.

"It was a sudden dizziness . . ." he muttered.

"Yea—a dizziness," said Ildico, and went quickly, with no more than a flash of her great eyes at the emissaries of "Estyloh."

"Thy dizziness hath now gone, Manour?" asked Obarton anxiously. "Yea? Glad am I—though thine indisposition cost us dear, for it discomposed the beautiful Ildico, and we had no more than a glimpse of her. No matter. Thou art truly thyself again, Manour? Ah, that is good! One cup—then rest awhile!"

"So far, Bullo—good!" breathed Obarton as Manour reeled out.

"We have made it good—so far," answered Bullo.

An hour later, at dusk, Attila and his swarm of killers, drunk with fire, murder, outrage and rapine, raged home.

Obarton and Bullo looked out from a window on the town-destroyers as they came in, and they did not like what they saw in the red and smoky glow of many torches.

"Head hunters and scalpers, I see!" said Obarton in a whisper as they stared out at the shouting mob of horsemen milling about the great square before the palace. "May the gods forever keep them out of Rome!"

"Cold steel for that," grunted the poison Professor. "The gods aid only those who aid themselves! Cold steel—or, better still, that which I carry in my pouches! Given my way and a reasonable sum and I could lay them stiff as ra . . ."

He broke off as Manour entered to report that Attila would view the Arabs in the morning. Meantime Obarton and Bullo, envoys of the Sheik, were invited to the wedding feast. The ceremony—quite a brief one—was even now taking place, and—they would not forget the matter of the chestnut mare with the white foreleg?

"Fear not, Manour—she shall be thine," said Obarton. "Come what may, she shall be thine." He had to raise his voice to make himself heard above the yelling devils in the square outside—who had already overslaked their thirst after their long ride, and were now shouting their besotted approval of the marriage.

"They would shut as loudly if it were a burial!" said Obarton, staring out.

Bullo's wide, thin-lipped, viper mouth moved.

"That, too, they may be shouting for ere many hours have sped!" he said in a malevolent whisper. "Gods! How they swill! I have seen nothing in our saturnalia so swine-like. Would that the Emperor ordered *me* to deal with these Huns, and furnished me the gold to get the simple things I needed! I would carpet this region—nay, this whole land—with a carpet of dead Huns such as the eye of man hath never seen!"

The poison Professor's eyes were glittering with a strange and sinister lust.

"Peace! Peace!" soothed Obarton uneasily. "One thing at a time, comrade!"

They waited, staring out, till a sudden roar arose outside.

"The ceremony is over—such as it was!" he said.

"We go now?"

"Nay—Manour will return to conduct us!" said Obarton, staring out. "Saw ye ever the like, Bullo?"

As far as the eye could reach flared the torches and fires of the Huns. The night was wild with flame, delirious with shoutings of men, the neighing of horses and the red gloom reeked with the odour of half-burnt horseflesh. Here and there the red light quivered on naked steel, brandished in the nightmare ecstasy of some of the barbarians, and the shrieks or the shrill screaming laughter of the women punctuated all. Men went galloping recklessly bound for far fires, forms glided darkly by as the crafty ones stole through the throngs intent on secret designs, slaves tottered under the vast weights of drink looted from a thousand ruined towns.

"And *this* no more than Hunnish revelry!" said Obarton, a fastidious if not a moral man.

"Bah! Would I were butler this night to them all!" deplored the Professor at his elbow.

Then Manour entered—half drunk but civil.

"He is in a good mood, and is desirous to see ye . . ." said the Master of Horse. "Be restrained—flatter him—bend well the knee—be humble and, above all things, flatter him!"

They nodded, smiling at the ignorance which hinted to a Roman of the value of flattery!

"And forget not the chestnut mare!" muttered Manour. . . .

They made no mistakes when, presently, the Master of Horse presented them to the Moloch of those days and his bride.

Inflamed by many things as he already was—including Ildico, brilliant at his side—Attila was still capable of a little further inflammation by Manour—who described the Arabs as an introductory to the presentation. The bow-legged old ruffian knew how to describe horses, and the bloodshot blackguard at the head of the long tables knew how to appreciate them.

"It is good. To-morrow we will try these horses. If they are all that our Master of Horse claimeth I will enrich ye so that ye can fetch me yet more of them. And now, drink and feast and make merry, Envoys, for ye have come at a good hour!"

Manour steered them to seats among the Hun generals, not far from Attila—and the feast was on.

It was not much of a feast for Romans, but it seemed a treat for the Huns.

Obarton and Bullo were careful at first, but they soon perceived that care would not long be necessary. There were no epicures nor gourmets present. All were just plain swallowers to a man. They gorged till they were stupefied, then set themselves seriously down to the business of lifting themselves out of their stupefaction with stimulants. This is not, and never has been, possible.

Obarton and Bullo gave a masterly impersonation of all present but, as they told each other afterwards, the thing was easy. Nobody was noticing them an hour after the feast began. Attila was little better than the rest of his "court."

It is to be remembered that at this period the Huns were relaxed. They had no serious war on hand—and there was not a vestige of risk that anyone in Europe was likely to attack them. In the field of war they were, for a time, deadly formidable—no man, no king, no general, dared despise them. In peace they were swine. . . .

Then, at last, Obarton and his lethal friend saw Attila, a short, thick, swarthy brute, attempt to rise, and, aided by Ildico's strong, white arms, succeed. He glared about him with glassy, bloodshot eyes, the veins on his temples standing out like ropes, his wet lip-corners dragging down, but his whirling mind could discover no cause of offence among the multitude of sots, and so he allowed Ildico and another to assist him away.

The eyes of Ildico flickered over the crowd and lingered for a second on the two Romans. Then she was gone.

They waited a little, seeming to drink. All around them the Huns were dropping like ripe berries, and they saw that they could go without attracting attention.

So, each with an arm around the other, hoarsely howling an entirely meaningless song, they reeled out. . . .

Throughout all that remained of the night their luck held—or they held it.

Ildico's luck held—or she held it.

The luck of the Europe of that day held—or was held for her by these three people, some Arab horses and a few horsemen.

But the luck of Attila, the Hun King, ran out forever that night. . . .

By the time the Hun guards, uneasy at the over-long silence in Attila's bridal chamber, dared to break in next afternoon, Ildico and Stylo were in the remote glooms of a distant forest among the gypsies from whom they originally came.

And Obarton and Co. were racing for Rome.

. . . . .

The Princess Honoria was lying fretfully on her couch well sheltered from the intense glare of the sun outside when her favourite eunuch ventured to announce that Obarton the Arranger was awaiting audience.

"Bring him forthwith," she said.

Her eyes gleamed as the Arranger came in.

"Draw nigh!" she said in a low voice. "Nay, closer!"

Her voice sank to a whisper.

"Thou hast come to report! Hast thou aught to report, Arranger? I have fretted bitterly through the long nights, the dreary days, lacking word from thee, silencing mine ears to the myriad rumours that wheel about the city like the pigeons of the air! The eyes of the Empress Placidia are dark with menace, the eyes of the Emperor, my brother, are full of boding, and rumour follows rumour. It is said that Attila draweth in his armies about him to march on Rome and take me at the sword's point! It is said that he hath sent envoys to Rome charged with tales to my discredit! Lies—lies—lies—they crawl the streets like asps! It is said that they have sent for the pallid Virgins of the court of Theodosius among whom I languished so long—that these may bear witness against me! Lies—asps! Tell me!"

She sat up suddenly, thrusting out a bare arm, to grip with jewelled and lovely fingers the wrist of Obarton.

"Tell me! Hast thou done aught for me?"

Her eyes were blazing.

"Tell me, I say! *What* hast thou done for me?"

She watched a slow smile dawn on the cruel, handsome face of the Arranger like one fascinated.

"Forget forever thy fears, thou beautiful one!" said Obarton, softly, leaning to her. "Attila is dead—dead—of a burst artery! This I swear—for I contrived it!"

She drew her breath in a sigh so long that it was as though it could never cease. But at last she returned the smile of Obarton.

"I believe thee, Obarton, thou most seemly of men! . . ."

She relaxed, thinking. Her lids fell, as if she were about to sleep.

Obarton the Arranger waited.

Then a whisper—

"Draw close the curtains—close; turn the key in the lock of the door. Speak low. I wish to talk to thee . . ."

He went over to draw the curtains, and as he glanced triumphantly over the city the rays of the afternoon sun struck upon his eyes with such an intolerable brilliance that he shut them for a second. The curtains swished together, but did not altogether shut out the light.

He opened his eyes again . . . on Mr. Hobart Honey's electric fire in twentieth-century London. It was glowing nicely.

So was Mr. Honey.

The Lama's pill had short-circuited just once more—that was all.

For a long time Mr. Honey stared at the electric fire. Then he poured himself a port.

"Pity!" he said. "Though perhaps it was just as well. I wonder how it finished! No need to wonder, really. Can guess for myself—men like me—like I was—usually came to a pretty uncouth finish in those days. Yes. Better off as I am! In a way. Though she certainly *was* a very attractive woman! . . ."

COMMENTARY

ON

THE ADVENTURE CALLED DEATH TO THE HUN

My friend Honey began to read the foregoing presentation of his affair with Princess Honoria, Attila the Hun, Bullo the Poison Professor, and Ildico, with great interest, which seemed to me, watching him, to merge slowly into intense irritation, markedly tinged with disgust. When he finished he threw the typescript on the table with a gesture of contempt. Then he picked it up and re-read the end again. But that only served to intensify his gloom.

"I suppose one has to accept it as a fair portrayal of me as I was—but I confess to feeling an impulse to protest against it. You have depicted me, Bertram, as a person devoid of all decency. Surely, my dear fellow, surely . . .?"

I shook my head.

"It is a photograph of the account you gave—not an imaginative picture. All I have added is a certain amount of good coarse humour—coarsish, say. Even as you requested me to do. It *is* true, of course, that, as Obarton you seemed to be devoid of the qualities which, nowadays, are usually recognised as essential to the make-up of a really typical 'good citizen.' Against that, however, it may —or may not—be set to your credit that you were extremely handsome in, I imagine, a sinister sort of way, and that you possessed (like Lord Scamperdale) a certain amount of 'low, ret-ketcher's cunning' which seemed to serve you well—at the time. But it would have been inartistic and inexact to have presented you, in that incarnation, as the type of man which is likely to be a winner of the Nobel Prize. No, Hobart, much might be lost by departing from the truth in these accounts—and it is certain that nothing can be gained. It has frequently occurred to me—to take several points of view—namely First . . ."

"Oh, for God's sake, not a lecture, Atkey, not a lecture! —Here, help yourself, and stop talking!"

I stopped talking.

BERTRAM.

THE FIFTEENTH PILL

THE FINAL FORAY

HOBART HONEY left the Censorship office in which he war-worked late on the third Christmas Eve of the war—so late that he invigorated himself all the blacked-out way home with the thought that he deserved all he could get during the rest of the Eve in question. The streets were full of slush, and the air was full of fog—as was Mr. Honey by the time he reached home. He had that day been censoring the outgoing American mail, and had run into a bunch of contracts addressed to film producers in Hollywood. These mainly concerned the sale of certain film rights of the plays of a famous English playwright. Judging from the grim legal safeguards of every known variety verbosely introduced into the enormous documents, the English playwright and his merry legal men appeared to labour under the impression that the celluloid Moguls of Hollywood were a kind of cross between playwright-eaters, tanks out of control, and devil-fish. Hollywood's legal representatives, for their part, seemed to be absolutely certain that the playwright was partly a ravening cannibal, partly a half-starved vampire, probably a born thief, and, in his spare time, doubtless a mad highbinder. So they protected themselves against each other accordingly—and Mr. Honey had been reading scores of pages of such protection all day, just to make sure that the whole thing was not some new and deadly form of Nazi threat against the United Nations. It is understandable that he waded home through the slush and fog as fast as he could, ate his dinner, visited the port decanter enthusiastically, and, well-established in his arm-chair before his fire, swallowed one of the Lama's pills as quickly as possible. He was in just the mood to return to one or other of his earlier incarnations for a spell.

His mind cleared rapidly. Nowadays he slipped from his life in the twentieth century to that in any other incarnation with the smooth easiness of a wet eel swimming down a fast river.

In a few seconds he was no longer Hobart Honey, of London. On the contrary, he was re-visiting an incarnation in which he was Sir Baldur de Huhne, formerly a knight of the court of the great King Arthur. He had never been actually a member of the goodly company of the Round Table—but he had been on the waiting list. Actually he had sat at the next best—the Oval Table which was as far above the Square Table as the Round was above the Oval.[1]

Sir Baldur de Huhne had long outlived these glorious days. He had been but a dashing and unprincipled youth in Arthur's day—but now Arthur and most of his knights had moved on into later, and probably better, incarnations, leaving Sir Baldur and a few others in the rear. If not an old man he was far from young, and now that knighting had largely died out as a profession he was, like the few knights remaining, finding it hard to make a living.

[1] Knights not entitled to any of the above tables sat on the Royal Floor.—Bertram.

He was sitting in the practically unfurnished hall of his practically demolished Castle, with a quart vessel of hard cider in his hand, staring thoughtfully at a few sticks smouldering in the practically burnt-out fireplace. He was incompletely sober—but the knights of his period usually were. He was not wearing his armour at the moment—that was standing in a corner supported by a post. Its mouth, or visor, was open, and it, too, looked incompletely sober, and seemed to be leering at him in a coarsely confidential sort of way.

Sitting on his haunches before the fire was Sir Baldur's spotted gaze-hound, Six-Leopards, gazing at his master.

But Sir Baldur de Huhne did not notice his armour or the gaze-hound. He was busy doing his accounts—in his head, for he could not write.

His calculations were not accelerated by the presence of a lady of certain age though with the remnants of great but slightly acid beauty, who sat in a ramshackle chair on the other side of the fire. She was asleep—but she was talking in her sleep. Talking pretty frankly. And when she was not talking she was grinding her teeth. Sir Baldur did not pay any attention at all to the sleep-talk of the lady—he got all of her conversation that he needed when she was awake. Nor did the grinding of her teeth distract him—he was always ready to admit that she had, on the whole, excellent reason to grind them.

She was the Lady Yeolande Blanchemains Iseult Lynette de Luxe de Laine de Ruffe. She did not actually look all that, but appearances are deceptive. Once she had been a Maid of Honour to Queen Guinevere, but that had been a long time before. She was now *châtelaine* and cook-housekeeper to Sir Baldur de Huhne. She had eloped with Sir Baldur at about the time Guinevere had eloped with Lancelot—the day after de Huhne had all-but jousted the head off of Sir Roderic de Ruffe. It was at the period when King Arthur's Court was in sore need of the overhaul which it never received, and it is a noticeably small exaggeration to say that Knights and Dames and Demoiselles were eloping all over the landscape in all directions.

Several times since then the Lady Yeolande and Sir Baldur had drifted apart and drifted together again. They had stayed put this time—neither had the money to leave the other, though each had the inclination. The vast possessions once owned by Sir Baldur's ancestors had shrunk now to a few acres of poorish land and the huge Castle had long been in ruins. It consisted now mainly of holes and corners. For forty years Sir Baldur had suffered from squander-mania—though he was now cured. He had nothing left to squander. The farm was not very productive, for it was badly tilled and understaffed. It was worked by two idle serfs—who were paid by results. They had produced no results recently on account of not having been paid for some earlier results.

So that the Knight and his Chatelaine would have been deeply ditched but for the spasmodic efforts of their servitor—an elderly person called Merlin who was outside splitting firewood while Sir Baldur was drawing up his balance sheet. Merlin also was a come-down. He dated back to the hey-day of Sir Baldur and the Lady Yeolande at the Court of King Arthur. He had slithered up to the castle of the King one day, arrayed in a black bombazine dressing-gown with silver moons, stars, crescents, triangles, circles, bars and ordinary blobs all over it, red shoes curled up at the toes, and a long black beard, and announced that he was the Foremost Magician in the world. He stated, briefly, that he was so full of magic that it hurt him holding it in. Most people believed everything they were told in those days. The awed sentries called the Captain of the Guard, a fat and purple man o' the world, overful of wine, mead, beer and ignorance, to whom the Magician repeated his story. It failed utterly to impress the Captain of the Guard—and he said so loudly, so loudly indeed that the guard turned out (after a fashion), a crowd of troops gathered, and quite a little bevy of lovely ladies craned their charming necks over the battlements to see what was happening. Among these was Queen Guinevere, who was taking a stroll up there with the King and her boy friend, Sir Lancelot.

Presumably the quick eye of the old soldier took in his august audience, and he repeated his challenge to the strange self-styled Magician, very noisily indeed. He evidently saw himself promoted to Major before long.

"No man, magician or devil, approaches the King's Grace till I am well-assured of his quality!" he declared, excitedly. "Give me, therefore, a taste of this magic!"

(Afterwards, it was freely acknowledged that the man was foolish to talk in this way—everybody, in those days, knew that magicians were to be treated with the utmost respect.)

Merlin faced the Captain. Then he raised his right hand and drew off the glove. He pointed his finger at the Captain of the Guard, intending to perform some minor conjuring trick, no more. In those days the simplest conjuring trick of to-day was a major operation.

Merlin pointed his forefinger at the Captain—and the man dropped as dead as a snipe before the gun of a good snipe-shot. Apoplexy. It had been coming to him for months—years.

It was Merlin's luck that it happened at that moment. He moved his arm involuntarily, and half a regiment ducked out of the line of his forefinger. Pale with fear of the consequences, he threw up his arm, intending to swear that he had meant no harm to the man—and all the ladies dived backwards from the battlements into the arms of their lovers. Those who had no lovers just dived backwards. Queen Guinevere had to put up with Lancelot's arms, as the King had tripped and missed her.

Merlin, a quick-witted bluffer (considering the times), saw how it was, and slowly pulled on his glove and concealed his fatal forefinger in the bosom of his dressing-gown.

Then he walked round the body into the Castle. Every time he moved as much as his right elbow folk ducked.

The King fortified himself with a quart of old mead and gave him a gracious reception.

His reputation was established for the next twenty years. He was made Court Magician for life—on the understanding that he kept his right forefinger unloaded in the presence of the King and Queen—and Lancelot. . . .

But the years passed, times changed, and people got wise to Merlin.

In the end, they pitched him out. He had constantly given himself a hearty welcome, and had not saved a cent. He took up the patent medicine racket, and travelled the country with his celebrated cures for rheumatism and more intimate complaints in people, glanders in horses, hydrophobia in dogs, and despair in jackasses. But he was getting old, and we are told that an old man's business never prospers. *His* didn't, anyway. In the end he was glad to take the post of odd-job man about the place at Baliheu Castle, the residence of Sir Baldur de Huhne.

He was out in the yard while Sir Baldur figured, Lady Yeolande ground her teeth and the gaze-hound, Six-Leopards, gazed. Six-Leopards was claimed by the Knight to be quite comfortably the best gaze-hound in Wessex. In a way, this was true—though good judges were in the habit of maintaining that the technique of Six-Leopards was faulty. The gaze-hound proper, they insisted, should always be on the watch or lookout or, in fact, on the gaze for deer.

Six-Leopards, they agreed, gazed well, but never for deer. Some said he gazed for food, some said he gazed for affection. He got very little of either, but he still went on gazing his blank, mournful, completely unintelligent gaze, usually at his master, sometimes at Sir Baldur's old falcon, which, as a rule, sat on a broken spear over the mantelpiece. It was moulting. Sir Baldur never went hawking nowadays, and the falcon had long ago forgotten how to hawk, anyway. It seemed to be always moulting. Once Merlin had undertaken to reawaken the spirit of enterprise in the hawk, and had taken the bird into the fields in order to let it stoop at a few fat partridges. The gaze-hound had gone with them.

But it had been a failure. A covey of partridges had risen, and Merlin had shouted "*Heu! Heu!*" and lifted the hawk high in the air so that it could stoop at them.

But the bird had merely started moulting on him. Six-Leopards had gazed sadly at the hawk, the hawker and the horizon—and they had all returned to the Castle, short of partridge. Perhaps it was because of a tendency of these old sporting memories to intrude on his mind that Sir Baldur's figures did not work out to show any result but sheer Insolvency.

But more probably it was because, with a startling suddenness, the Lady Yeolande shouted in her sleep:

"He shall make an honest woman of me yet!"

She made the statement so loudly and violently that she woke herself up, and drew the gazes of the startled Knight, and his gaze-hound, and his moult-hawk instantly upon her.

Her rather bitter eyes fixed themselves on Sir Baldur. "*You*, I meant!" she said. Evidently her dream had been vivid.

"Why, yes . . . if possible," he agreed. "But, Yeolande, permit me to ask when I have made a dishonest woman of you? Was it in the days of the Round Table? When you were wife to the good Irish Knight Sir Roderick de Ruffe? Whom I slew. Was it when you whipt me away with you into a region which you called Wonderland? I have wondered mightily about that for years—in Wonderland. I have put the question to myself these many times. I have said—'It is for her to make an honest man of me—if she can. But she cannot!'"

He utilised the cider vessel again.

"Wit ye well, Yeolande, you cannot make an honest man of me, I cannot make an honest woman of you, for we are both naturally dishonest. There was a time when I grieved for this. But I observed that my grief did not change the facts. Therefore I ceased to grieve—and concerning . . ."

He was rambling on when Merlin entered without any ceremony whatever.

"The pig is dead, the horse refuses to work, there is disease in the bee-hives, and I am well convinced that the serfs have stolen most of the oats. Thus, fair sir, there will be neither bacon nor ham, no honey from the hives, nor a sufficiency of porridge for our winter provender!"

The Lady Yeolande uttered a sharp exclamation of sheer dismay.

"The pig dead? What has caused him to die? What have you been doing to him? This is ruin!"

Merlin stared at her with a water-eyed dignity.

"Doing to him? Doing to him? Forsooth! What should I be doing to my winter meat but waiting upon him hand and foot these months past! But pigs do not thrive upon air and water alone, and woundily little of that! The creature died of sheer lack of enthusiasm for a life in which there was not half enough, nay, nor quarter enough to eat!"

"Why did you not cast a spell or an enchantment upon him, so that he took a happier outlook on life?"

"Good lack, lady, I have long forgotten the difficult art of casting spells, and enchantments do not serve as a substitute for barley-meal!" said Merlin sourly. "I am no longer a working magician—I am a retired one!"

The Lady Yeolande was really agitated.

"But, pardie, I cannot provide the meals in this establishment unless I get the raw material therefor. I am utterly undone!"

"Probably it is not the first time you have been utterly undone—nor I—nor Merlin. Yet we survive!" said Sir Baldur, a little muzzily.

He stared at them.

"It comes to this," he stated. "I must make a foray. Other knights do!"

"A foray! 'Swounds, what kind of a foray do you think *you* are capable of making?" snapped Yeolande.

"I shall show you!"

He turned to Merlin.

"Fill my tankard—and fill one for the Lady Yeolande—and one for yourself while you are at it!" he commanded.

"One sees why the cider sinks low in the barrel ere ever the winter is upon us!" said Yeolande sourly—but she did not refuse.

"Nay, nay, but we are in evil plight. It is no time for parsimony. We go now into conference, thou, fair Yeolande, Merlin, and I. And it is necessary to well stimulate our brains. Therefore let us not be niggard of a couple of gallons of the acrid and belly-griping fluid which we call cider, God wot!"

Merlin, nothing loth, forayed himself to the cellar, muttering. On the broken spear the hawk, its head so sunk in between its shoulders that it looked neckless, moulted silently; the suit of rusty armour looked more intoxicated than ever; and Six-Leopards gazed vacantly at Sir Baldur.

The hound irritated the Lady Yeolande.

"Oh, sally forth into the fields and catch yourself a rabbit, imbecile!" she said.

But Six-Leopards merely twitched a shapeless, pendulous ear and shrugged a loose-jointed shoulder. He knew better than the chatelaine that there was nothing in the fields to eat but grass—and not too much of that. The serfs had long ago devoured all the rabbits.[1]

Sir Baldur got up and went over to look at his armour.

"Humph! Merlin must polish it—if he has any polish," he said.

"Yes, and oil the joints—if he has any oil," sneered Yeolande.

"Also, he must mend the spear! And sharpen the battle-axe!"

He stared round.

"Where *is* the battle-axe?"

"In the wood-shed—where it hath served for many years!"

"Hah! It is time and overpast that we had an alteration here," said Sir Baldur.

"That is right sooth, and I recommend you to make the same, for albeit so late in the day . . ." began Yeolande, but broke off as Merlin tottered in with a very large quantity of cider indeed.

When their brains were well stimulated Sir Baldur spoke briskly.

"First, the horses!"

[1] The rabbit is usually considered to be something rather special in the matter of increasing and multiplying—but the Baliheu rabbits could not keep up with the appetites of the Baliheu serfs. They were exceptionally voracious serfs.—Bertram.

"Horses—why horses?" enquired the Lady Yeolande. "Is it your design to take Merlin?"

"I deny not that the times are woundily scant, but there are some appurtenances which no knight can dispense with. A squire to ride behind me I must have!"

"The Horse will refuse to carry both you and Merlin!" said Yeolande, deliberately. "Probably he will refuse to carry one of you—for he is becoming fanciful, querulous and crabbed in his old age."

"*I* will deal with The Horse," said Sir Baldur. "And as for my Squire we must contrive."

He took a long soop at his cider. Then his eyes brightened.

"I have it. You shall borrow from our neighbour, Sir Maravaine le Gros, his great mule. He will deny you nothing, Yeolande—and the loan of his mule will not totally wreck his fortunes, strained, like mine, though they may be!"

"Oh, I doubt not I may contrive that!" said Yeolande carelessly. "But ere you equip the foray would it not be the better strategy to decide whither you purpose foraying—and what for?"

"That is well spoken, Madame," said Merlin, wiping his beard with the back of his hand. "For wit ye well, fair sir, what shall it profit you to mount The Horse and me the mule and ride forth trusting to chance? It needs a goal, a destination, an object!"

"True, true!" Sir Baldur nodded rather irritably. "So think of a goal, an object, Merlin! *I* cannot think of everything!"

Merlin took it slowly—by degrees.

"This is a desperate venture," he said. "And much consideration must be given unto it. Let us begin at the beginning—only thus shall we fare smoothly unto the end. Our object, fair sir, is money."

"That is well put, Merlin," agreed Sir Baldur. "Money. Whither shall we wend to acquire it?"

"First we must ascertain where there is Money or Treasure—and go thither."

"Right again, Merlin."

"There is the root of the problem! Part One—*where* is Money—or Treasure?"

Sir Baldur nodded.

"I begin to see your line of reasoning," he said sagely. "First find out where money is—point one. And having found out where it is then—point two—we go and get it?"

"Yes," said Merlin with the air of a man who has solved a serious problem.

Sir Baldur drained his tankard.

"*How* shall we get it?" he proceeded.

Merlin drained *his* tankard.

"That is Point Three of the problem—and must be dealt with when we arrive at the place where the money is!" explained Merlin gravely.

The Lady Yeolande drained *her* tankard, and put it down with a crash.

"If it is your desire to see a good woman go raving mad before your eyes," she shouted, "keep on talking for a few more seconds just exactly as you are talking now! Pardie, you are like two crows on the bough of a dead tree in a black frost discussing the worms asleep out of reach under a foot of frozen soil! Look you, this is no case for a flux of words—this is a case for action. I will speak plainly, for time is short and the need is desperate! Upon this foray, so-called, depends the continuance of my presence here. Succeed quickly and I remain—fail and I go to a place where a good *châtelaine* will be appreciated at her worth—Sir Maravaine le Gros has long desired such a *châtelaine* to control his establishment—and I doubt it not that he will be overjoyed to . . ."

A sudden exclamation from Merlin, who had been muttering absent-mindedly into his beard, stopped her.

"By Excalibur, I have it! The Treasure of Sir Bustyr de Fysshe!" he cried.

They stared at him like gaze-hounds.

"If, by good hap, we may once lay hands upon this treasure, then shall our griefs and troubles vanish like the morning vapours that dissolve under the rays of the rising sun!"

"I have not heard of that treasure," said Sir Baldur. "Where is it to be found and, by good fortune, won by the victor in a trial of arms? Sir Bustyr de Fysshe—de Fysshe!" he mused. "Yes, I have heard of him these many years past. Tell me, Merlin, is he not a short, thick, swarthy man of mine own age, who bears upon his shield three dogfish *argent*, a cat-fish *azure*, a lobster *gules* and a couple of cod-hooks sinister?[1] Methinks that many years ago I ran a course with him in a tournament at Camelot and jousted him into hospital for several months!"

"That is verily the self-same knight!" said Merlin.

Sir Baldur stood up and stretched, accompanying himself with a hiccup or two.

"Should be easy to pick a quarrel with him, as between two knights, and joust him into hospital again. Have done it once—should be able to do it again."

"You are not so young as you were—nor so sober——" Yeolande warned him, "sometimes!"

He stared.

"Nor so sober sometimes!" he echoed. "I can amend it! 'Swounds, unless I come down upon this man's treasure and that right soon, meseemeth I am doomed to be sober for all my days hereafter!"

He sat down again and fixed a rather wandering and watery eye on Merlin.

[1] This is what is called "heraldry." Very difficult.—Bertram.

"Tell me more of the treasure of Sir Bustyr. Where doth he keep it? Is it locked away in deep cellar? In steel-barred cell? How is it guarded? Is it much? How do we come at it?"

But Merlin shook his head, clawing at his grizzled beard.

"Nay, fair sir, I know not. No more I know than that it hath come back to me, a memory of the past days when all the secret news of the kingdom trickled through to the King's Own Magician. The Treasure of Sir Bustyr Fysshe. I seem to hear again the words in these ancient ears. By your good leave, Sir Baldur, it is in my mind that we fare forth nigh unto the City of Sarum, outside of which, I mind me, is the domain of the Fysshes. There we may abide making patient and subtle enquiry concerning the treasure. Then, when we have discovered where he keeps it hidden away . . ."

The Lady Yeolande broke in.

"Tarry awhile, Merlin, and make clear to my mind the following—is this an adventure of knight errantry or is it to be an ordinary burglary?"

"Burglary!" snorted Sir Baldur. "Not so! Am I not a knight? Is it not the correct, nay, the only decent thing for me to challenge Sir Bustyr to attempt some small deed of arms upon me, and when I have vanquished him to require his treasure for ransom? That is the rule to which all knights are bound, and may dogs howl on the cowardly hound that shrinks therefrom!"

Six-Leopards threw up his head and howled like a wolf till Sir Baldur smote him sore and silenced him.

"He thought I was talking about him, the intelligent animal! He is very quick—he shall accompany us on this desperate adventure!"

Six-Leopards heard and crawled behind the arras—evidently not an enthusiast about desperate adventures.

For many hours and more tankards they discussed it. In the end the knight and Merlin fell asleep.

The Lady Yeolande stood up and looked them over. "Knight and Squire! Huh!" she said, and ground her teeth a little. "Unless my mind most woundily miscarrieth I see my finish! *Châtelaine* to Sir Maravaine the Fat! Bah!"

She ground a little more, snapped her fingers, looked to see if there was any cider left, found there was not and so went to bed.

The men slept on, the fire burnt low, first mice, then rats came out to play about the hall, Six-Leopards, the gaze-hound, stayed quietly behind the tattered arras —he was nervous of rats—and over the mantelpiece, motionless on the broken spear, the hawk continued to moult in absolute silence.

. . . . .

Ten days later The Foray started in earnest. Compared with what a foray by Sir Baldur de Huhne had been twenty-five years before this was little better than something, a fragment, that had fallen off a circus in a poor way of business.

First rode Sir Baldur on The Horse—an elderly, sneering, grouchy carthorse, of no beauty whatever, whose distinguishing characteristics were bone-idleness and low cunning. Sir Baldur was wearing several parts of his armour—all of it that was not rusted out or broken. His vizor would not shut, but that only made him look as if he was having a hearty laugh at things in general. The feathers at the top of his mild-steel bonnet drooped a little, but that was the fault of the moths. It would not be seemly to blame a knight for what the moths had done to his feathers. He rattled as he rode a good deal, but, after all, armour that did not rattle was like spurs that did not jingle—frightened nobody. The Knight's personal outfit was, then, shabby but genteel—shabby-genteel, call it. He would have looked better if Merlin had used a little more metal polish on him. But they had run out of polish. Still, Sir Baldur had been a pretty hot knight in his day, and, like a retired professional time-serving soldier of these days, he had not lost the hall-marks. One could tell that, though he was out of practice, well past his prime, and definitely on the down grade, he was, in a way, the genuine article. He sat upright and kept one hand quite imposingly on the sword hilt at the top of the scabbard clanking by his side. It would have been a good guesser who guessed that there was no blade left under the hilt. The battle-axe wasn't bad considering its years of honourable service in the woodshed.

Six-Leopards, the spotted gaze-hound, shambled alongside, looking sick of the foray already, and sicker still of himself. He was not really a brave dog nor an enduring one, though Sir Baldur, without much conviction, claimed him to be both. A man must be loyal to his dog.

Riding behind, on Sir Maravaine le Gros's mule, was Merlin, looking like a fool—as he himself grumbled. He had dug up out of an amazing collection of junk which he had amassed for himself in one of the bat-haunted, belfry-like upper attics an armouring consisting of what looked more like a tattered chain-mail shirt with the tail missing —a "model" which had once been very popular among knights who wanted something a little more flexible than the heavier, showier, jointed and riveted armour. It did not suit the ex-magician very well, but, in a limited sort of way, it protected him from the ears down—the hat consisting of chain-mail which hung like curtains down over his hairy ear-holes.

He carried Sir Baldur's spear and shield—the latter a triangular affair upon which was painted a yellow beehive with blue bees carting honey to it from all directions, and the motto "*Huhne non jam*"—a bit of hideously inaccurate and ignorant Latin which obviously was intended to express the slogan, "Honey, not jam!" Behind him, various more useful but less decorative articles were slung—a kettle, a pot, a stone jar and some parcels of victuals. By and large, a good big load. The mule did not seem any too well satisfied about it. But then that mule never was, and never had been, satisfied about anything whatsoever. He was what a mule-and-ass psychiatrist would have classed as a frustrated mule—and this in spite of the fact that he usually got his own way in most things, for he was also a fighting mule. Also a kicking and biting one. He was a blackish-brown brindle, with a totally hairless tail that looked like indiarubber. His name was Rosamund—which means Rose of the World.[1] By any other name he would have smelled as fragrant.

Sir Maravaine le Gros, who came over to see them off, and was standing at the door with the Lady Yeolande, bethought himself of an omission just as they started.

"Hey!" he shouted. "The Squire has forgotten Thunderbolt, the falcon. For his dignity's sake Sir Baldur must have his falcon, man!"

"Thunderbolt cannot come upon the foray," bawled Merlin.

"Why not?"

"He's moulting!"

"Oh!" said Sir Maravaine, and said no more till they were out of sight. Then he turned—all the eighteen stone of him—to Yeolande.

"Whither go they—and why?" he asked.

[1] In those days of romance they were oddly careless about the gender of the creatures they christened. The King, for instance, had a rather pretty little cow called Jack. Queen Guinevere owned a peacock which she named Matilda. Sir Lancelot had a thundering great red bull which he christened Nelly. That sort of thing. Malory forgot to mention this in his chronicles—so I have done it for him. Malory doesn't mind.—Bertram.

"Alack, Sir Knight, the treasury of the good Sir Baldur hath dwindled low. Now he sallies forth to challenge Sir Bustyr de Fysshe to knightly combat. If it befall that he knocketh out Sir Bustyr then naught shall serve for ransom but the whole of the treasure of Sir Bustyr—of which doubtless thou hast heard rumour these many times!"

The fat Knight thought.

"Yea, fair Yeolande, I have heard rumour of the Treasure of Sir Bustyr. But it had never occurred to me to sidle along to Sarum and take a flyer at it. Am somewhat too big-about these days, alack!"

"Yes," said Yeolande, eyeing him thoughtfully. "Indeed I fear that your *embonpoint* would get somewhat in the way!"

They both sighed.

"The times are very hard on we knights of old!" he complained. "But there is still to be found a cup of cider—no?"

"Yes," said Yeolande, and led him to it. She glanced at him sidelong as they went.

"And wit ye well, Sir Maravaine," she said. "I, speaking for myself, I am not averse to a reasonable *embonpoint* in a knight. Seen in silhouette meseemeth it stabilises a man!"

Sir Maravaine seemed glad to hear that. . . .

. . . . .

For a long time The Foray progressed in austere silence through a rather cold, heavy rain which began to fall when they were rather too far from Baliheu Castle to make it worth while turning back. Moreover, it was The Horse and Rose-of-the-World who felt the impact of the climate most severely. Sir Baldur was, in a sense, indoors out of the weather—so, of course, was Merlin, except that there were more leaks in Merlin's chain-mail than in Sir Baldur's armour. Both were turning bright red with rust—but neither cared. Six-Leopards walked under The Horse gazing at the mud. He was a good gaze-hound, but he was afraid of rain. The Horse went onwards, sneering—he did not appear to give a damn for anything as long as he could sneer about it. But with Rosamund it was much otherwise. He mooched along under Merlin seeming as meek and resigned as an aged cow. But he was not so. Slowly, and very gradually, as the muddy miles passed, his enormous ears left their usual angle and—unlike those of The Horse, which merely drooped—shaped themselves flatter and flatter to the fiddle skull of the animal. Merlin noticed this. He also noticed that between his shanks the mule seemed to be swelling up, becoming more and more virile and electric—like a battery on a charging bench.

"There is evil toward. It accumulates—like lightning!" muttered Merlin apprehensively—not quite knowing from whence or whereunto it was accumulating. But some subtle instinct informed him that evil was in his immediate neighbourhood.

But, in spite of these things, the general reception accorded to The Foray by such of the public as were abroad in that inclement weather did much to raise the morale of the Knight (and Squire) of Baliheu.

Whenever they saw a party coming they pulled themselves together. Sir Baldur hauled on The Horse's jaw till the unfortunate animal's neck curved like that of a Greek war-horse, and himself sat up in the saddle straight and stiff and rode sternly by with his hand on the sword-hilt; Merlin held the great spear pointing straight up to the sky and flaunted the great shield well to the fore—with a *Huhne non jam*, take it or leave it, air; Rose-of-the-World merely flattened his ears a little flatter and showed his black, yellow and green teeth as he went by—still stewing up his amperage.

The met parties usually took one glance and hastily removed their hats (if they had any) and bowed to the ground nearly humbly enough to satisfy a stockbroker. Or else they got off the road into the ditch and bowed there. Or, if they were young and nimble, they hopped over the hedge and departed from the neighbourhood at a right smart clip. Knighting—for poor knights—may have been out of fashion, but there was still a great number of people who remembered the customs of the knights of King Arthur's day. After all, it was not considered servile or cowardly or wretched or small or lousy to duck into the ditch or kneel down in the mud with your hat off and apology for living written plain all over you when an iron-clad knight, probably as lousy as yourself, passed by with a battle-axe in his right hand, his left hand on his sword hilt, and a Squire with a horseload of further implements, tools and weapons behind him. It was generally held to indicate that, on the whole, you were publicly expressing your personal prejudice to continue living all in one piece—instead of being distributed in several portions over the immediately adjacent landscape.

This was the Age of Romance—and one had to pay close regard to one's step in those days.

They came to an inn—a humble affair, built of mud and wattle, with some pigstyes built of wattle and mud at the back.

Sir Baldur pulled up and read the signboard—which merely announced to all comers that the proprietor was Gulph, and that he was licensed to sell "Beers, Wines and Spirits."

Sir Baldur broke a window,[1] and the innkeeper ejected himself from the inn, bowing about two-thirds flat to the ground.

[1] Not glass, in those days, of course, but the thin skin of some creature's intestines stretched to the point of transparency. We use it for sausages nowadays.—Bertram.

"Varlet, what hast thou in thine hovel fit to serve to the most goodly knight in all Christendom—none less, God wot, than the great Sir Baldur of Baliheu!"

"Beers, wines and spirits, may it please your Grace!" babbled the innkeeper, apparently half paralysed.

"Set them forth, set them forth—one double order of beers, wines and spirits!" bawled Merlin, as good a Squire as one could require. "And haste thee, haste thee, varlet, lest a goodly knight, weary from sore conflict with the cannibal infidel on thy besotted behoof, should parch him this day!"

"Now, Heaven forbid!" croaked the innkeeper—and set them forth.

The beers were flat and flatulent, the wines were acid and the spirits were low to the point of melancholia.

The Foray consumed them, discussing their plans, and rode on.

Nobody hit the innkeeper. This appeared to be regarded by all, including the innkeeper, as payment generous to the point of over-tipping.

The next people they met (in a way) were two small-business thieves. They saw the thieves lurking in the rain by a gallows tree about two hundred yards ahead.

When they reached the gallows tree there were no thieves there. There were two black dots far across the fields that looked like two crows flying rather rapidly over the furrows. . . .

Next they ran full tilt into a knight in black armour evidently out on strict business.

Six-Leopards left them temporarily there—he was rather afraid of dark knights.

They halted face-on and studied the heraldry on each other's shields as these were advanced by the Squires.

Sir Baldur did not know the first three letters of the alphabet, but he understood heraldry. The dark knight's shield was jet black all over, and upon it was painted in white two wickets silver, three skillets blue, four mullets red, five gullets pink and a watermelon gold, the whole surrounded by a *fesse dancette.*

"It is *not* possible!" said Sir Baldur. "This knight is an illusion!" He passed on.

"No, sah! I'se no illusion—but ah suah am glad to be on mah way!" said the dark knight, and passed on also. Foreigner, evidently.

Both seemed glad to pass.

Six-Leopards rejoined them—hind foremost—out of a drain into which he had taken a look.

Then, gradually leaving behind them the wolf-haunted wastelands, the dark forests wherein things rustled and squealed and outlaws prowled like leopards, they passed through a region where the slovenly fields showed signs of a rude tillage, improving as they progressed.

The further they went, the greater the improvement, till suddenly, when the afternoon was well-advanced, they perceived that they were in a fair land.

At the top of a steep hill, Sir Baldur suddenly stopped The Horse and gazed out over a region of corn and cows, of sheep and fat hogs rooting, lost in genuine admiration.

"Now, by Excalibur, here is a land of which these eyes have never seen the like!" he exclaimed.

Merlin muttered agreement.

"We draw nigh unto Sarum," he said. "This is that land enriched by the Treasure of Sir Bustyr de Fysshe. No man but a master of treasure unlimited could so conquer and subdue the savage soil of our land, Sir Knight!"

The rain swept clear across the land, the last great shadows of the cloud swung off the corn as they stared, and the sun illumined the whole lovely green and golden countryside.

Sir Baldur, thinking of his own starved acres, sighed.

"Yes—treasure is needed for this!" he said. "Capital—no man may so transform the face of this uncouth earth lacking capital!"

They turned into a track which took them along the side of a field in which a serf was working. This person, peremptorily questioned, told Sir Baldur that he was indeed upon the lands of Sir Bustyr de Fysshe, and with a boldness very unusual in a serf, added in a very obsequious tone indeed, that Sir Bustyr was a very great knight, with but one slight prejudice—namely, a dislike, amounting almost to a horror, of having strangers riding over his land.

"That might well be for the common folk," said Merlin haughtily. "It is not intended to apply to so mighty a knight as my master!"

A vast voice from behind promptly corrected him.

"Art wrong!" it bawled. "The prejudice is especially directed against such as thou and the knight thou art squiring from the back of thine evil-smelling mule. We want no strange knights and squires hanging around the fields. Quit them, therefore, and that right soon, lest an ill thing befall ye!"

It was a short, broad, swarthy man, with a rather uneasily hectoring manner. There was a curious quality of sham or imitation fury about the general delivery of his abrupt invitation to quit. It was almost as if his wife was listening to him, having first set him at the strangers.

"That, fair sir, is but a churlish fashion of address to the noble and distinguished knight . . ." began Merlin—but he was promptly interrupted.

"Knight! Knight! We need no knights loose in this parish—especially so-called noble and distinguished ones. Better the crows—they come less expensive about the place. This is a farm, and a good and a great one, and we have no time for foolery. Therefore, get off the farm!"

The Foray hesitated.

"Knight! Knight!" continued the man. "They are behind and far behind the times! Good lack, these useless ironclads but encumber the face of the fair earth! I, too, was once a knight in the days ere I was instructed in the error of my ways! Hast never heard of the great Sir Bustyr de Fysshe—he who overthrew and brake and smote forty-seven knights on an afternoon at the tourna——"

But here he seemed to catch a sound from the little wood behind him, and changed his tone abruptly.

"Get off this land, I charge thee—and now—forthwith! Thou, in the ancient iron suit—and particularly thou on the mule!"

He rushed forward, raising his agricultural-style cudgel, a severe-ish looking bat to use for the simple purpose of mule-starting. He brought the cudgel into contact with the mule in no half-hearted fashion—an error in tactics.

All day long Rosamund, notoriously the most evil-tempered mule in Wessex, had been stewing and steaming up his amperage, and he was just about fully charged when Sir Bustyr, the knight-turned-farmer, made contact with his club.

It was all over in a matter of seconds. Rosamund slewed half round in a peculiar, writhing motion, and Merlin departed from the saddle in an involuntary hurry. Then, freed of his load, the mule whirled on Sir Bustyr, and with uncanny speed and absolutely fatal precision, kicked the blustering farmer clean out of this incarnation before the man could possibly have realised that he had cudgelled the most dangerous member of The Foray he could have selected. He had intended to start Rosamund off his land—instead he had automatically started himself on a new incarnation.

The serf rushed up with a spade, but Rosamund whirled on one hind leg to face him, and the serf altered his direction, changed gear up and headed for the horizon, leaping everything that got in his way.

Sir Baldur clanked off The Horse and helped Merlin up. Then he took a look at Sir Bustyr.

Merlin shook his head.

"Fair sir, he hath been in Valhalla this five minutes!"

He was pale.

"Little I dreamed what I have this day bestridden. I have been riding a catastrophe—not a mule! Thus ends our quest for the treasure of the late Sir Bustyr even ere it be well started!"

"Be not so sure thou speakest that which is sooth!" said a grim voice behind them. They turned quickly to see, striding from the little path through the wood, a lady.

She was of middle-age, and she looked, talked and acted like a strong and steely man.

She stood there studying them for many minutes. Her hard eyes took them in from head to foot and back again.

"Yes, it is even as the innkeeper sent word! 'Fore God, ye are, of all the knights and squires in Christendom, the very lousiest I have set eyes upon. Thou, Sir Knight, art the rustiest thing in armour I have seen these many years —come out of it ere thou rustest completely up!" Her glare swept on to Merlin. "And as for thee, thou poor, depraved wretch, thou hast no tail to thy shirt! . . . Nay, bandy no words with me, nor proffer me lies. I have had word of ye and of the purpose for which ye came. Ye spoke too freely of your evil plans at the inn, and all your words have been reported to me, the mistress of these fertile domains. Deny it not—ye came here to win away the Treasure of Sir Bustyr de Fysshe! Look around upon these fat and profitable lands, upon the flocks and herds, the corn! And know that I, the *châtelaine* of Sir Bustyr, —who, poor man, was as ignorant of the art of husbandry as doubtless thou art—I transformed his starved and untilled lands into this. I—the Lady Violente la Sterne—*I, who for that reason and for none other, am known far and wide as The Treasure of Sir Bustyr de Fysshe!* And I am not yet buried treasure, wit ye well, Sir Knight!"

She laughed harshly.

"Now Sir Bustyr has left me lone—aye, I saw it all. An accident—no need to protest—I saw all. Had he but been a better judge of a mule he would never have approached that wild animal. Yet it is thy fault, Sir Knight, that I am bereft of an obedient and docile friend for whom I have managed these many years, and whose estate I now inherit. Now, I am minded to hand ye both over to the King's troops, who are encamped beyond yonder hill under command of mine own blood cousin—short shrift for treasure stealers have they—if suitably rewarded! . . . But I am a merciful woman—I will first *see* thee, Sir Knight."

She turned to Merlin.

"Get him out of that armour and right quickly!"

There was a rasp in her voice that made Merlin jump. Obligingly enough, Sir Baldur dismounted—rather stiffly, and after sore trouble Merlin got most of his metal off him.

The Treasure of Sir Bustyr looked him well over.

He was not so young as he had been, but, for his age, he was not a bad-looking old blackguard. And there is many a good tune played on an old fiddle.

Her hard face softened just a shade as she studied him.

He twirled his moustache at her.

"Thy name, Sir Knight?"

"Sir Baldur de Huhne of Baliheu!"

"Art wed, Sir Baldur?"

He bowed deeply.

"Nay—a single man, Lady Violente!"

"Hast means, Sir Baldur?"

"No means, Madame, beyond my horse, my hound, my hawk and a ruined castle! I stand alone!"

"I, too," she said. "Thy coming has bereft me of mine only friend," she added slowly.

He stared.

"*Well?*" she asked impatiently. "Art a chivalrous knight—or not? Am I not the Treasure of Sir Bustyr? Am I to live the rest of my life alone? Why camest thou here? Art not so bright as I thought thee, Sir Baldur! In plain English, what art thou going to do about it?"

He looked at her, thought of the troops over the hill, and reflected swiftly. He had forayed all the way from Baliheu for the Treasure—here she was before him. A little masterful and undoubtedly a strict, even severe, lady. A knight would have to watch his step—there would be only one boss about the place if he stepped into the shoes of the unfortunate Sir Bustyr—and it would not be him.

Still—she was inviting him to marry her—a woman of quick decisions, and one who knew her own mind.

He did not hesitate. There was no way out even if he did hesitate.

"Nay, but it were over-bold, Violente . . ." he began.

"I like a man to be bold—sometimes," she said. "At other times he need be but obedient and docile, and interfere not with the farm—Baldur!"

He dropped on his knees and proposed to the Treasure in true knightly style.

He was accepted. (Just as well for him, for, as he learned later, the Lady Yeolande had already left Baliheu for good with Sir Maravaine.)

"Thy squire—dost need him, Baldur? I like him not—he hath a hang-dog look?" asked the Treasure.

"Wilt abide with me, Merlin—or wouldest prefer that I give thee Baliheu and all within it? I do not return—nor do I need it now!" said Sir Baldur, who already had a shrewd idea that Yeolande had taken care of herself.

Merlin did not take long to make up his mind. He had made but a very moderate hit with the Lady Violente and knew it.

"A knightly gift, fair Sir Baldur—accepted in the spirit in which it is proffered. Doubtless I can make me a living out of it!"

"Mayest have The Horse also, Merlin!"

"Now God be praised for that, Sir Baldur—had walked back else, for never will I again bestride yonder catastrophe."

"Well said! So ends as goodly a venture as ever knight launched upon. Farewell, Merlin!" said Sir Baldur, and turned to the new life—and a new wife.

"Short and sharp—but that is the way of it nowadays, my love," said Violente, who had been issuing orders to a gathering of serfs concerning the late Sir Bustyr. "Come then—home!"

She spoke truly, for a few seconds later Mr. Honey was back at home—but in his London flat. Once more the Lama's pill had shorted on him just when a new life looked before him.

He took off a port, thoughtfully.

"Not quite the quality of knight I might have been," he said at last. "But doubtless there were worse ones."

There was a certain amount of comfort in that—cold comfort, but still, in a way, comfort.

COMMENTARY

ON

THE ADVENTURE CALLED THE FINAL FORAY

"Ye-es," said Hobart rather reluctantly—in a grudging kind of way—after he had read my account of the "foray," "Ye-es, it could have been something like that—well, it *was* like that. You have not flattered me——"

"It was not designed to be an effort at flattery, my dear Hobart. I worked on the material supplied by you faithfully, I believe!" I replied.

"Eh—oh, yes, yes, quite. I don't deny that. I don't even mean to criticize," he claimed, handsomely enough. "But for just a moment I was a little startled to realise again how extremely sordid the whole thing was. You have a remarkable gift for illuminating the sordid, Bertram. Quite how you do it, I don't know. It's not quite the kind of illumination one—somehow—perhaps unreasonably—expected—it's a—a species of marsh-gas, fungoid—if you follow me—phosphorescent-toadstool illumination—with an odd, probably unhealthy, odour!"

"Thanks," I said, dryly. "I agree entirely. You are not favourably impressed by the local atmosphere of the affair. Neither was I—but I could not allow the odour of the thing to affect an honest attempt at faithful reproduction!"

He thought that over—still glancing here and there at bits and pieces of the typescript.

"Yes—you are right. I have no really good reason to object. After all, we were a good deal as you have shown us. Quite a lot of the knights of the period were at that time badly on their uppers, as the hatefully vulgar saying goes. The standard of living was tragically low. There wasn't a bathroom in the entire kingdom, nor a carpet. The cooking just wasn't cooking—it was heating edibles. Clothes, too—there has been a fearful amount of nonsense written about the clothes of the period. Even we knights. There was practically no underwear. Hence the long, trailing skirts. Even Guinevere—when she unhooked her beautiful gown it just fell at her feet and she was ready for bed. There were no nightclothes. And the armour—you know, Bertram, it was terrible stuff. The quality of the iron was deplorable—steel, as we understand steel, wasn't invented. . . . Yes, they were rough times—very rough. And illiterate. . . . Yeolande actually did do that—left me flat for Maravaine."

His eyes grew absent in the old familiar way.

"Once she had been quite the loveliest woman at Arthur's court. And yet, curiously enough, it was not on her account that I slew her husband, de Ruffe. It was about quite another girl that we fought. Ruffe was tough. At the time we fought I had never met Yeolande. Indeed it was at his funeral that I made her acquaintance. Yes, she was lovely in those days—but fickle!"

He smiled.

"You chose to be facetious about Six-Leopards. Probably you are right—he was not a really good gaze-hound. Good pedigree, though. In-bred, probably—weak in the intellect. Six-Leopards was perhaps a rather grandiloquent name for him."

"Two-Leopards would have been enough?" I suggested.

"Ample!" agreed Hobart.

"Did the falcon Thunderbolt ever stop moulting?" I asked.

"I don't know—I remember nothing that happened after I turned to go to the house of The Treasure."

"Probably you had a moderately good time. You needed a managing woman to look after you. No work.

Plenty to eat and drink. And a determined woman to keep you steady. It might have been worse, Hobart."

"Yes," he said, "and it might have been better!"

He sighed, and reached for the decanter.

"Will you have a drink?" he invited.

"No, thanks—I don't drink," I said.

BERTRAM.

TAILPIECE

So much, then, for this the first book of the adventures of Hobart Honey—*how* much I do not know and shall not until the royalty statements, showing how much I am in debt to the publishers, arrive.

Meantime, readers, permit a few words of explanation. This book has been written with the sole purpose of making you laugh at a period in the world's affairs when a laugh is priceless. If it succeeds in doing this, then I have done you good—if it fails, then I have done neither you nor myself much harm. No literary merit is claimed for the tome—none was aimed at. The critics may tear it to shreds and devour them—if they like; or they may accept the thing in the spirit in which it has been offered and try to get a smile or two for themselves out of it—if they can. It's all one to me now, for the work is done, and I can presently run through it and try to discover a laugh or two for myself. I need it. I trust no one's corns (or prejudices) have been inadvertently trodden upon. When one sets out to produce humour of the particular kind aimed at in this book it is absolutely necessary to assume, at the outset, that it will be read only by completely corn-less people. If you are the proprietor of an abundant supply of corns it is regrettably certain that your laughs will be fewer than your scowls. If this proves to be the case, consult your conscience. Explore it frankly. You will probably discover that corns of the kind that can be inflamed by the mild chafing of a well-meant attempt to make you laugh are not the kind of corns (or prejudices) worth having.

For the rest, buy the book, read it, laugh at it and forget it.

BERTRAM.

THE END